When we got there the whole house was in flames. Seventy-five-year-old wood burns well, everyone knows that. Fire leaped from the rooftop, poured out of windows, roaring and crackling like a living thing. Three fire trucks were parked in the street; firemen aimed high-powered hoses at the flames, especially in the windows, but it was useless. Anyone could see that. Neighbors, wearing coats over nightclothes, clustered nearby, pointing, talking, worrying for their own homes. I wished the wind would carry embers across the street to the Collinses' roof; bastards, all of them.

I stared at the flames, like someone in shock, thinking . . . too bad Grandma wasn't inside, too. And then I worried, what if they'd gotten out? What if they didn't die? "Mom? Dad?" I cried, jerking away and bounding toward the burning house, but Mr. MacDonald grabbed me. "They're gone, Brian. I'm terribly sorry. The firemen said they couldn't get to them, too much heat and fire. . . ."

I threw my hands over my face and made like a grieving son, shoulders heaving and all that, but I was thinking—wow! I did it, really did it. Smart planning is how—every step, even tonight's sleepover with dorky Andy MacDonald. It was so easy. And no one could pin it on me. At last, I was free. Free to leave this dumb college town where I don't fit. Free to live where I want, where I always wanted to live—in California. No more parents conspiring about their weird son, watching my every step, doubting my every word, sending me to still another shrink, and talking about sending me away to a place where they'd straighten me out. *For my own good. Their* own good, they meant!

They got what they deserved. . . .

The
Killing
Boy

Gloria D.
Miklowitz

Bantam Books

New York | Toronto London

Sydney Auckland

RL 5.3, age 10 and up

THE KILLING BOY
A Bantam Book / December 1993

The Starfire logo is a registered trademark of Bantam Books,
a division of
Bantam Doubleday Dell Publishing Group, Inc.
Registered in U.S. Patent and Trademark Office and elsewhere.

ISBN 0-553-56037-9

Published simultaneously in the United States and Canada

Bantam Books are published by Bantam Books, a division of Bantam
Doubleday Dell Publishing Group, Inc. Its trademark, consisting of
the words "Bantam Books" and the portrayal of a rooster, is Regis-
tered in U.S. Patent and Trademark Office and in other countries.
Marca Registrada. Bantam Books, 1540 Broadway, New York, New
York 10036.

PRINTED IN THE UNITED STATES OF AMERICA

RAD   0 9 8 7 6 5 4 3 2 1

Prologue

Brian

The digital clock read 2:37 when the phone rang. I'd been watching it since bedtime as it clicked forward a slow minute at a time. Waiting.

"Hello?" Mr. MacDonald's hoarse, sleepy voice came from the next room. "What? Oh, no! Yes, of course!"

I smiled and rolled over, pretending sleep. A moment later MacDonald rushed into the room and shook my shoulder. "Brian! Brian! Wake up!"

"Huh? What? Mr. MacDonald? What's the matter?" I rubbed sleepy eyes and sat up.

He loomed above me in a red plaid robe, hair all awry, eyes wide with shock. "Hurry, get dressed! Something terrible's happened!"

"What?" I stumbled out of bed, glancing at the clock. "It's after two!"

"There's been a fire, a terrible fire. Your home—your parents . . ." His voice broke.

"Fire? My parents? What do you mean?" I grabbed for my pants, avoiding MacDonald's eyes, getting that tone of fear just right. "Are they okay?"

"I don't know. Hurry! I'll drive you there." With that, he rushed from the room.

When we got there the whole house was in flames. Seventy-five-year-old wood burns well, everyone knows that. Fire leaped from the rooftop, poured out of windows, roaring and crackling like a living thing. Three fire trucks were parked in the street; firemen aimed high-powered hoses at the flames, especially in the windows, but it was useless. Anyone could see that. Neighbors, wearing coats over nightclothes, clustered nearby, pointing, talking, worrying for their own homes. I wished the wind would carry embers across the street to the Collinses' roof; bastards, all of them.

"Oh, Brian. We're so sorry, so sorry," Mrs. MacDonald said, trying to comfort me with a hand around my waist, a touch that made me almost flinch.

I stared at the flames, like someone in shock, thinking . . . too bad Grandma wasn't inside, too. And then I worried, what if they'd gotten out? What if they didn't die? "Mom? Dad?" I cried, jerking away and bounding toward the burning house, but Mr. MacDonald grabbed me. "They're gone, Brian. I'm terribly sorry. The firemen said they couldn't get to them, too much heat and fire. . . ."

Mrs. MacDonald let out a terrible cry.

I threw my hands over my face and made like a grieving son, shoulders heaving and all that, but I was thinking—wow! I did it, really did it. Smart planning is how—every step, even tonight's sleepover with dorky Andy MacDonald. It was so easy. And no one could pin it on me. At last, I was free. Free to leave this dumb college town where I don't fit. Free to live where I want, where I always wanted to live—in California. No more parents conspiring about their weird son, watching my every step, doubting my every word, sending me to still another shrink, and talking about sending me away to a place where they'd straighten me out. *For my own good. Their* own good, they meant!

They got what they deserved. . . .

1

It started with a phone call almost a year ago.

It was Sunday, breakfast time. During the week we all eat at different times, but on Sundays Mom likes us to be together. She makes omelettes and fresh orange juice and the kitchen is steamy all morning from waffles baking. I always go out and bring in the Sunday paper, which weighs half a ton, so I can pull out the comics and sports section before anyone else.

The phone was ringing when I got back in the house. "I'll get it!" Dad called, halfway down the stairs. He was barefoot, needed a shave, and was dressed in his usual grungy Sunday best—torn jeans and an old T-shirt. I went on into the kitchen, dropped the classifieds in the recycling bin, and brought the rest of the paper to the table.

Mom looked up and smiled. She was bent

over Cookie, pouring maple syrup on her waffle. "How was the party last night?"

"Fine." I glanced at the headlines on the sports page, then turned to the comics.

"Any nice girls?"

I rolled my eyes.

"Not telling, huh?" She wiped Cookie's mouth and sat down. "Was *Gina* there?"

"Mo-om!" My face began to burn. I never should have told her about Gina because now she asks about her all the time. When Mom was working she never had time to pay much attention to me. But now that she's home she's gotta know everything. Where I've been and who I talked to, and what I think—everything! Who needs it? It was better before.

"Well, *was* Gina there, Tim?" Mom sat down and leaned toward me, a teasing gleam in her eyes.

"Yes!! Now, will you leave me alone?" I jumped up and went to the waffle iron, glad to be able to turn my back so she wouldn't see my face.

"First love. How sweet." Mom sighed but suddenly her voice changed. She glanced up. "What's wrong?" she asked.

I flipped a waffle onto my plate and turned around. Dad looked sick. He dropped into his chair and put his hands over his face.

"Daddy's crying. Don't cry, Daddy!" Cookie

said. "Want some?" She offered a forkful of dripping waffle.

"Shh, Cookie. Just eat your breakfast." Mom turned back to Dad. "Honey? What's wrong? Is it your mother?"

Dad shook his head and finally took his hands away. "It's Pete and Linda." His voice sounded funny, like it hurt to talk.

"Pete and Linda, what?"

"That phone call . . . it was from the police in New Haven. I can't believe it. They're dead." Dad looked up and his eyes filled with tears.

"Dead?"

I almost dropped the plate and hurried back to the table. Pete was Dad's brother, and Linda his wife. They lived almost three thousand miles away. Uncle Pete taught political science and Aunt Linda did something with computers. They had a son, my cousin Brian. Whenever we went East Brian seemed to be off at camp or with a school group touring Russia or someplace. I'd only really met him twice.

"Oh, my God! Oh, honey! I'm so sorry!" Mom took Dad's hand. "How? What happened?"

Dad shook his head as if he couldn't bear to say the words. "Fire! Can you believe it? Fire! They burned to death in their own home!" He covered his face again and for a while all I heard was deep muffled crying.

I tried to imagine what it might be like burning to death, trapped by fire everywhere, trying to get out of the house and not being able to. I shivered.

"What about Brian? Is he okay?" Mom asked, a catch in her voice. "Oh, God. How awful! Was it the wiring? It was an old house. They don't smoke! How did it happen?"

"I don't know. *They* don't know. They're investigating. Brian's okay, thank God. He was staying overnight at a friend's house."

"Thank heavens! Poor child. He must be devastated!" Mom said.

My cousin was a few months older than I, almost sixteen, a big guy, but to Mom still a child. How awful it must be for him to lose his parents. As often as I get mad at Mom or Dad for getting on my case, I'd never want them dead. Poor Brian. What would happen to him?

From the corner of my eye I caught Cookie drowning her almost empty plate with syrup. Mom was too busy to notice. I reached across the table, gripped her hand tight, and wrenched the bottle away. She whimpered, looking to Dad for support. "Cookie!" I warned in as menacing a tone as I could. "Go to your room!" She squirmed away as I tried to wipe her sticky fingers. "Caroline!" She knew I meant business when I used her real name. One last whimper and she slid off her chair and was gone.

"The funeral's day after tomorrow," Dad said. "I want us all to go. For Brian's sake, especially.

He's all alone, except for my mother. We're the only family he's got."

That one phone call would change our whole lives. How could we have known it?

The next day we flew into New York and rented a car to drive on to New Haven. It was eight P.M., eastern time, when we finally checked into our hotel. While Mom unpacked and I kept Cookie busy with a book, Dad got on the phone to Grandma.

"I understand." I heard him say. "If you're not up to it we'll see you tomorrow. I'll have the limo pick you up at nine. Was it the wiring? Uh-huh. He talked about replacing it. Why isn't Brian with you? Mom? Did you hear me?" I don't know what Grandma answered but Dad said, "Don't cry, Mom. I'll call the MacDonalds now and we'll work something out."

He phoned the people Brian had stayed with and asked how my cousin was doing. Dad nodded and bent into the phone. "I see. He's probably in denial. Hasn't sunk in yet. We'd like to see him as soon as we can."

"Read book," Cookie said, shaking me back to attention.

"Brian will be here in a few minutes," Dad said when he hung up. "The MacDonalds say he's taking it pretty well, considering. Tomorrow. . . ." Dad's Adam's apple slid up and down. "Tomorrow—will be very hard for him, for all of us."

"What's going to happen to him, Dad?" I asked. "Does he go to an orphanage, or something?"

"An orphanage? Of course not! He'll be coming back to live with us."

"He will?" The words came out of my mouth in a squeak.

"Right. Any objections?" Dad frowned, eyes challenging.

"No. No! Of course not!" I said real fast, but I wasn't so sure. Another person in our family? A stranger? Even if he was my cousin, I hardly knew him. This would change everything. Where would he sleep? What if we didn't get along? Still, he *was* family, and almost my age. Maybe it would be okay having someone else around for Mom to mother; take the pressure off me. It might even be nice having a guy my age to hang around with, like a brother. Yeah. By the time Brian knocked on the door I was feeling pretty good about the idea.

Brian looked great. He was tall, well built, and fair with dark hair and gray-blue eyes—the kind of guy girls go for. I thought immediately of Gina and worried that he could be trouble.

He held out a hand and smiled, real polite and gentlemanly, like he'd gone to military school, which maybe he had. "Tim, hi. Nice to see you again," he said.

"Hi," I said, stumbling for what to say next.

"Sorry about your folks." Mom came forward, hands out.

"Brian ..." She wrapped her arms around him and mewed at him like he was a hurt child, except he was a man, a good foot taller than she.

Dad came forward and patted his shoulder. "Good to see you, son. Come, sit down. We have a lot to talk about." Dad motioned to a couch and chairs near the window. On the table between them was a basket of fruit and a box of cookies family friends had sent up.

Dad and Mom sat on the couch and I perched on its arm. Brian took a chair opposite and helped himself to a cookie. "These are good." He nodded appreciatively. "Lots of nuts. Oh, excuse me. How thoughtless!" He held the box out to us. "How was your trip?"

He sounded so normal, like we were all here for a visit, not his parents' funeral. In his place I'd probably be gulping down tears, blubbering. Maybe that's what Dad meant about denial. What happened hadn't sunk in yet.

Mom took a cookie out of politeness, I think, and exchanged looks with Dad.

"How did it happen, Brian?" Dad asked gently. "Do you have any idea?"

"A fire. They think it started in my bedroom, right next to theirs. Maybe the space heater." He shrugged. "If I'd been home I'd have been the first to go."

"Oh, Brian!" Mom cried.

"It was some blaze! Nearly lost the house next door, too."

"About tomorrow, Brian. Do you have any clothes? I imagine everything you owned was destroyed. Do you have anything suitable to wear to the funeral?" Dad asked.

Brian nodded. "I'd planned to go to church yesterday with Andy and his folks so I took along a suit and stuff. They're at the MacDonalds'."

"We'll see that you get them. We thought you might like to stay with us tonight. That way we can all leave together for the services. How do you feel about that?"

"Fine with me." Brian helped himself to another cookie. "It's going to be strange, saying good-bye." His forehead wrinkled and for a moment I thought he might cry. "I'll miss them." He reached for an apple. "Uncle Bill? Dad said if anything ever happened to them you and Aunt Barbara would take care of me. Is that true?"

Dad reached across the table and put a hand on Brian's arm. "Of course. Of course we'll take care of you. Won't we, honey?"

"No question!" Tears welled in Mom's eyes.

"We want you to come back with us. It will be wonderful to have another son. We always wished we could have given Tim another sibling closer to his age."

Brian turned to me as if he needed my approval, too. "Tim?"

I thought how I'd feel in his place, alone, having to count on strangers—even if they are related. I swallowed a lump in my throat. "It'll be great having another guy around so Mom won't be on my case all the time."

Mom gave me a playful whack on the knee.

"Well, gee, thanks!" Brian said, smiling at us. "I know Dad left money for me, but it's not money I care about. It's family! You're all so great to take me in. I'm all choked up. And going to live in California! I can't think of any place I'd rather be."

2

Dad had taken an adjoining room for me and Cookie. Instead, Brian and I shared that room and Cookie slept on a cot near Mom and Dad.

I was really bushed and I could hardly wait to hit the pillow. Brian, on the other hand, seemed wired, though it was already one in the morning.

He settled on one of the two double beds, lotus fashion, and bent over the newspaper while I went into the bathroom to wash up. When I came out he said, "Yeah, it's here. Look!" He turned the paper so I could see an article about the accident. "Yale Professor, Wife, Die in Tragic Fire," the headline read. There was a picture of Uncle Pete at a blackboard. Brian had the same strong face and good looks, but lots more hair.

The article told all about my uncle—how he

became a full professor at thirty-two, published a lot of important papers, and lectured in countries all over the world. The paper also said that my aunt had recently been promoted to assistant director of the computer center. I guessed my cousin might be something of a brain, too, with parents like that.

I handed back the paper. It didn't seem fair—two good people wiped off the face of the earth—just like that. "Nice article," I muttered. "Your parents were pretty terrific."

"Did you read to the end? Did you?" Brian sounded angry. "See how that reporter spelled my name? With a 'y' instead of an 'i'? Dumb creep." He dropped back on the bed, hands under his head, lips pressed tightly together and stared up at the ceiling.

I climbed into my own bed and turned my face to the wall. I didn't know what to say. Mom once explained that sometimes people who can't handle a terrible loss transfer their anger to someone or something else. Maybe that's what Brian was doing—transferring his anger to the newspaper reporter. Poor guy. In his place I'd probably be crying like a baby.

I must have slept, five minutes maybe, maybe an hour, when I awoke with a start. It took me a moment to figure out where I was. Something was wrong. A light flickered, casting a dancing shadow on the wall beside me, and a sulphur smell burned my nostrils. I bolted upright, my heart banging loud enough to hear. "Brian!" I shouted. "What are you doing?"

My cousin sat on his bed just feet away, lighting matches. He seemed completely unaware of what he was doing. I don't think he even heard me. He lit one, let it burn down to his fingers, blew it out, then lit another.

"Brian!" I jumped up and yanked the matchbook away, singeing a finger. I flipped the bed lamp on and glared at him. "You crazy? What were you trying to do, burn the place down?"

Brian stared at me with blank eyes and didn't answer.

"It's two o'clock in the morning! What the hell were you doing?"

"I was . . ." Brian started, then stopped and covered his face with his hands. "I was just trying to imagine what it was like for my parents. Trapped. The fire. The smell, the heat, screaming! Not being able to escape!" When he took his hands away his eyes had a strange, excited glitter. "I saw it all. I stood outside and saw the house go up. The firemen couldn't get near them. I saw it!"

I shuddered and almost reached across the space between us to touch his hand. "Hey, you burned yourself. I'll get something!"

"No, no; it's all right." He covered his fingers with a hand, still staring at me.

"Listen," I said, earnestly. "You can't torture

yourself. Sometimes terrible things happen for no reason. It's not your fault and there's nothing you can do about it. Try to get some sleep. You gotta get up soon and it's gonna be a pretty tough day."

"Yeah," he said softly. "Right." He lay down and crossed his arms over his eyes. "Listen. Do me a favor. Don't tell anyone, okay? Your folks might think I'm nuts, and I'm not."

He studied me through his fingers.

"Sure."

"Good."

I turned off the lamp and sat on the edge of my bed, waiting for the adrenaline to cut off. The acrid smell was still so strong I was surprised the smoke alarm hadn't sounded.

Was my cousin a nut case, or was this just a shock reaction? What were we getting into, bringing him into our house? I stared at my cousin's dim shape in the darkness and listened to his regular breathing. Did I dare go to sleep with a firebug in the next bed?

I left my bed and went to the chair where Brian had left his clothes. With only the bathroom light to see by I went through the pockets of his pants, shirt, and jacket. No matches. Relieved, I tiptoed back to bed and hid the matchbook I'd grabbed from him earlier under my pillow. It took a while for me to fall back to sleep.

In the morning, the night's incident seemed less serious. I felt a little foolish making so much of it, chewing Brian out like that. Big deal, lighting matches. How many times had I done the same?

When we joined my folks and Cookie in the hotel coffee shop I could see Mom's approving glance at Brian's appearance. But though he looked fine, my cousin seemed withdrawn. "Sleep well, boys?" Dad asked.

I glanced at Brian and said, "We slept just fine, Dad. Right, Bri?"

"Right," he echoed. He turned to Mom. "Aunt Barbara? What about Grandma? Won't she be with us today?"

"Of course, dear." Mom pushed her uneaten breakfast aside. "We talked with her last night. She's taking it hard. We told her we'd be bringing you home to live with us."

Brian watched Mom over the rim of his juice glass with a kind of impersonal curiosity. "What did she say?"

"Well, she was upset, so I can't remember just what she said, exactly. But losing you, too, has to be very hard on her. After all, you've been close since you were born. I'm sure she'd love for you to stay and live with her, but she's getting on in years and she knows the best thing would be what your parents wanted—that you come stay with us."

"She doesn't like me."

"Oh, Brian, dear. That's just not true," Mom

said. "She wants you, but it's just very hard for someone her age to bring up a teenager."

Brian smiled.

Mom glanced uneasily at Dad. "Let's go over the schedule for today," Dad said, changing the subject. "The limo will pick us up in about an hour. Grandma, too. The funeral home has arranged for us to have some time alone with . . ." Dad choked up, cleared his throat, and added, "to say our good-byes. After the service we'll . . ." He went over everything that would happen.

I'd never been to a real funeral, only funerals for my pets when they died, so all of this was new and kind of interesting. Before the service our family sat in the chapel, apart from everyone else. An organist played sad music while my aunt and uncle's friends took seats. The minister said a lot of nice things and then other people came up to the microphone to talk about Aunt Linda and Uncle Pete. Grandma sat between Mom and Dad, crying softly. Mom dabbed at her eyes and Dad took deep gulps of air. Brian stared at the flower-covered caskets, hands tightly clasped. I stared at them, too, imagining the charred remains of my aunt and uncle, thinking of how it must have been for them in those last minutes. Poor Brian. What a vision to live with for the rest of his life.

A reception followed the burial. It was held at the MacDonalds' house and everyone who'd gone to the funeral came. "Stay close to Brian," Mom had whispered. "He needs someone his own age right now. Try to keep his mind off his sorrow."

It didn't take much trying. The dining room tables overflowed with food people brought. Brian stacked a plate with little sandwiches, cookies and nuts, poured himself some punch, and said, "Let's go find a place to sit and watch the hypocrites."

I stifled a grin, filled my plate, and followed him into the living room. Maybe he did sound disrespectful, but he was right. All around us were people with long faces when they talked to Dad. As soon as they found the food they stuffed their mouths and looked for friends to joke with.

"Brian . . ." one lady cooed, coming up to us. She opened her arms as if she expected him to jump up and fly right into them.

"Mrs. Foster . . ."

"My dear. Oh, my dear. What a terrible thing."

Brian gazed at the floor.

"We are all so sorry. So very very sorry. We all loved Pete and Linda."

"Thank you, Mrs. Foster." With great sincerity he added, "I appreciate your condolences." He started to get up. "May I get you some punch?"

"No, no, I'll help myself. I just wanted to say that when you come back to visit, we want you to be sure to call. Your parents were among our dearest friends."

"I will. I promise I will." There was a catch in Brian's voice, like he'd been really touched.

"Visit that old bag? Fat chance," he said a moment later. "I'd rather walk on hot coals."

I laughed uneasily. "Hey . . ."

"What's with you, Tim? Lighten up. Everything I say or do makes you wince. What a farce this is. Half these people were jealous of my parents. See that guy there?" He pointed to a man with a beard. "He's wanted to head the humanities division for years. With Dad gone, he's next in line. Think he's sad?"

I felt my face go red.

"Bet you always do the right thing, just what the teacher says and what your parents want, right?"

When I didn't answer he said, "You need someone like me around, someone to loosen you up a little, put a little spice in your life. You're going to be glad I'm coming to live with you in California."

Cookie sat between us on the flight home the next day. Brian played finger games with her and kept her amused with stories he made up about dragons and witches. It gave me a chance to catch up on the reading I had to do for English. But I couldn't really concentrate. My mind kept going back to what Brian said about me and I wondered if he was right. Sure, I did my share of chalking doors on Halloween and setting off firecrackers when I shouldn't, like that. But on the whole he'd figured me right. I was a good kid. Maybe too good.

I stole a glance at Brian, scaring Cookie so she'd have nightmares, scaring her the way kids love being scared, knowing I couldn't. Boring—that's what I was. Bor—ing. For the first time in my life I felt like a real wimp.

Yeah. With Brian around things would be different. I decided that I could use a little spice in my life.

3

"Is that smog?" Brian asked on the drive home from the airport. He peered out the window at the gray sky, the wispy fog moving in from the coast.

"Fog. May as well get used to it," Dad said. "Comes in about this time most days and doesn't leave till the sun burns it off around ten o'clock the next morning." Dad gestured to the left. "There's the high school you'll be going to, Brian. Tim's school."

I tried to see my school through Brian's eyes. Low buildings spread out over a big green carpet of grass. It looked new compared to the old brick school buildings back East. There were a few cars still in the student lot though it was already almost four.

"Dad said I could have my *own* car when I turned sixteen," Brian said.

My heart flipped. Brian getting a car? "See

Mom!" I cried. "Aunt Linda and Uncle Pete thought sixteen's old enough!"

"Not now, Tim! And not again!" Mom warned.

"They're always saying the insurance is too much for a teen male driver," I complained to Brian. "I told them I'm perfectly willing to work for it!"

"We don't want Tim taking time from his schoolwork at some low-paying job just to support a car," Mom explained.

"I could still keep up my grades. You know I could! That's so unfair!"

"You have a point, Aunt Barbara," Brian said.

"See?" Mom turned around. "Brian understands. Why can't you?"

Damn him! If he was going to be my ally, why didn't he support me instead of scoring points with Mom and Dad? I opened my mouth to protest but Dad said, "Drop it, Tim!" He stopped the car right in front of our house. "Well, Brian, here we are—your new home. Recognize the place?"

Still fuming, I looked out to the house I'd lived in since I was six, a two-story Spanish-style house like lots of others in the neighborhood. A big purple bougainvillea covered most of the southern wall and climbed over part of the roof. The gardeners were just pulling out of the driveway.

"It's a nice house, Uncle Bill. Real nice." Brian said.

"And it's your home now, too," Mom said. "We want you to feel part of our family."

"Is Brian my brother now?" Cookie asked.

"Absolutely, sweetie. Absolutely!" Mom said.

So I had a brother now. I'd always envied other kids with sisters and brothers to talk to and play with while I was an only child until Cookie came along. Still, you get used to it. I heard enough from friends to begin to see advantages: no pesky sibling to share a room with, to fight with over messing with your things, no smart-ass sister who gets better grades or macho brother to be compared with.

Now, like it or not, I had a stepbrother— someone I hardly knew but found intriguing and hoped to like. We'd have adjustments, sure, but it could be fun, too. With Brian around maybe Mom and Dad would let out a bit more leash.

My bedroom's big with windows looking out to the pool in back and to the house next door. Last year Mom went on a decorating spree. She bought me a new bedroom set—big Mexican-style chest of drawers, desk, and twin beds. She put in a chair and lamp for reading and *orange* spreads for the beds.

"So, these are our digs," I said, opening the door to my room, *our* room now. "This will be your bed. You can have these drawers, this part of the closet. Until you get some clothes, you can use whatever of mine that fits."

Brian surveyed the room and nodded. Then he went over to the window and looked out. "A pool. Nice." He opened the door to the small balcony and walked out. "Where's the dog? I thought you had one."

"Plato's at the kennel. We'll pick him up tomorrow. You ever have a pet?"

"A cat, for a while." He looked away. "He scratched me once, real bad. Left a scar. Want to see?" Before I could answer he unbuttoned his shirt and showed me a red line running from his chest to his stomach.

I walked over and touched it. "Wow! That's vicious! How'd it happen?"

"Who knows. Cats are so unpredictable."

"Where's he now?"

Brian rebuttoned his shirt and came back into the room. "Jumped out of a window. We used to live in a sixth-floor apartment."

"That's gross! Weren't there screens?"

"Yeah, there was a screen, but he shot right through, like a rocket! He went *splat*, like that!" He slapped one hand against the other. "Bye-bye puddy cat."

"Yuck!"

Brian nodded and wandered around the room, fingering this and that. He stopped in front of my model airplane display and picked up my B-52. It had taken months to build; I'd waited six weeks just for a special silver-gray paint that the hobby shop didn't have in stock.

He held the model at eye level and squinted at it, turning it this way and that. "Nice," he announced, nodding. Then he pretended to fly it, striding around the room, swooping it up and down, making noises like a plane in trouble.

"Hey! *Careful!*" I chased after him and grabbed his shirt. "Put it down, Brian! *Brian!* You're gonna break it! Give it to me!"

"Zoom!" he bellowed, almost shoving the plane in my face. Then, with a grin, he held it high over his head. "Will it fly? Let's see!"

It would break; he knew it. I got a sick feeling in the pit of my stomach. "Give that back, or else!"

"Else, what?" We stared at each other a moment, then he slowly lowered the plane and put it in my hand. "Had you there for a minute, huh? Come on, Tim. Chill out. I was just having some fun. You know I'd never hurt your little plane."

"Yeah, sure." Shaking with anger, I set the model back on its stand on the shelf.

"This your girlfriend?" Brian asked a moment later from behind me. "Cute."

I swung around to see him sitting on his bed, holding the framed photo of Gina I keep on my nightstand. She's standing near a tree, head tilted playfully, hands on hips. I guess I wouldn't have been so angry if it hadn't been for the B-52. "Just put that down!" I stalked over to the bed, grabbed it from him, and set it back on the nightstand.

He raised his hands defensively. "Jeez! What a temper! I was just admiring the cute girl. Who is she?"

"Gina. My girlfriend!" I glared at him. Gina would be expecting my call. With Brian around, there went my privacy.

"You want to phone her?" Brian asked, reading my mind. "That's okay. I'll just go downstairs, get out of your way." He strode to the door and looked back. *"Sayonara!"*

Alone, I frowned at the door. How to figure this guy? He threw me off balance.

Shaking my head, I dropped onto my bed and picked up the phone. I'd hardly begun to dial when suddenly the door swung open and Brian stuck his head in the room. "By the way, cuz— be sure to tell Gina I'm looking forward to meeting her." He grinned. *"Sayonara!"*

"Drop dead," I said under my breath as the door closed again. If that's what to expect from a "brother," who needed it? I finished dialing.

"Hello?" The tension faded when I heard Gina's voice. I could just see her, small and full of a kind of happy energy. She'd be in jeans and a T-shirt and her long, dark hair would be falling over one eye. "Hi!" I said.

"Tim! You're back! How'd it go? Was it too

awful? Is your cousin all right? Did they find out how it happened?"

"Whoa!" I said. "First, did you miss me?"

"You were only gone two days!"

"A whole forty-eight hours! So, did you miss me?"

"Uhhhh . . ."

"Gina!" I bellowed.

She giggled. "Well maybe—a little." She let me digest that for a moment, then rushed on to say, "I bet *you* didn't miss me at all, what with all the excitement. How's your cousin?"

"Brian? He came back with us. He's my roommate now." I dropped my voice. "Though I'd rather it was you."

"Yeah, yeah. Sure. What's he like?"

I turned over onto my back and closed my eyes. "He's tall. Dark hair, fair complexion, kinda nice looking. . . . Not as good looking as me, of course."

"Of course," Gina agreed.

"I guess an athlete, too. Football, Dad said. And I'm not sure I really like him."

"Why?"

"He's—so perfect. Neat. Says the right thing to everyone. He's won over Cookie and Mom already. But there's something. I can't put my finger on it yet. . . ."

"You're not just a little jealous, are you? Annoyed he's getting more attention than you? Be fair. It's got to be awful for him, losing his parents like that. Having to live with strangers . . ."

"Yeah. But he sure doesn't seem upset. He seems pretty cheerful to me."

"He's probably still in shock, poor guy. In his place I'd be a basket case. In two days he's lost everything—parents, home, friends. . . ."

"I don't think he has any friends," I said, needing to defend myself. "Not his age, anyway. There was a twelve-year-old he stayed with the night of the fire, *a twelve-year-old*! But no one his age was at the funeral."

"He *must* have friends. Come on, Tim, have some compassion."

I didn't answer. Maybe Gina was right.

"What about your grandma? She practically brought him up, didn't she? Think how he must miss *her*!"

A picture went through my head of all of us at the airport. The flight had been called and it was time to board the plane. Time to say good-bye to Grandma who had driven us to the airport. Daddy gave her a big hug. Mom kissed her. Grandma gathered me and Cookie into her arms and said she loved us. But where was Brian through all of that? Standing off to the side, watching. How come Grandma didn't hug him, too? Had I missed it?

"All I'm saying is that Brian seems a little strange, sometimes, but maybe it's just me. I'm not used to having a *brother* all of a sudden. I don't know what to expect."

"Expect the unexpected," Gina said from the experience of being the middle kid of five. "Like today. Do you know what Charlie did?" She went on to tell me about her kid brother who left his hamster in her dresser drawer.

I laughed, but suddenly I sat up and held the phone away from my ear. Someone was standing outside my door, listening. I could always tell by the creak in the floorboard. Would it be Brian?

In a voice louder than normal I said, "Brian wants me to tell you he's eager to meet you." I eased out of bed and tiptoed to the door, stretching the phone cord as far as it would reach.

"Well, isn't that nice!" Gina exclaimed. "Isn't that really nice! You can tell him I'm looking forward to meeting him, too."

"Hold on a sec!" I reached for the doorknob with my other hand. In one quick motion I yanked it open.

Cookie stood there, looking up, her big, innocent violet eyes hopeful. She clutched *Ira Sleeps Over,* her favorite book. I must have read it to her a hundred times.

"Want to see Brian," she said, peering around me. "Brian? Where is he? He promised! He promised he'd read book!"

4

"You're wanted in Mrs. Turner's office, Tim," Mr. Gordon said just after second period began. He turned back to the blackboard to work out the algebra problem he'd assigned for homework. I gathered up my books and left the room.

Mrs. Turner was the school counselor so I guessed it had to do with Brian. Mom said she'd be bringing him in to register, saying the sooner he got into a normal routine the better.

Mrs. Turner's a tall, pretty black woman, real no-nonsense. Talk to her for one minute and you feel she can read your deepest, darkest secrets. She drives a red Porsche convertible. Every morning before leaving the parking lot she covers it with a fancy canvas top, stands back a moment, and grins.

"She's waiting for you," the aide in the office said. "Go right in."

I knocked at her door and opened it at the same time. The three of them stood together as if the meeting was about over. Mom fished in her purse for her car keys and Brian extended a hand for Mrs. Turner to shake.

"It has been a real pleasure meeting you, Brian," she said, pumping his hand enthusiastically. "You have a delightful and charming nephew, Mrs. Anderson. And such a perfect gentleman. I'm very impressed."

"Why thank you, Mrs. Turner!" Brian placed a hand on his heart and bent at the waist. "*I'm* very impressed. You've given me such excellent advice and shown so much understanding. I can't thank you enough!"

I cleared my throat, trying to hide my disgust.

"Oh, Tim," Mrs. Turner said, recognizing me at last. Her dark eyes sparkled. "I'm appointing you Brian's 'big brother.' Show him the ropes—where his locker is, the gym, the cafeteria. Will you do that?"

"Sure."

"Well then, I guess we're set. Brian? If you have any problems, any problems at all, just remember—I'm here." She walked to the door and opened it. "Good luck. It was nice seeing you again, Mrs. Anderson."

Out in the hall Mom said, "Gotta go. Got a dentist appointment. Come right home after school. We've got to get Plato." She adjusted her shoulder bag. "Brian? You going to be okay?"

"Sure. Don't worry, Aunt Barbara. Tim's going to 'show me the ropes.' "

"Well then, see you guys later. *Sayonara*." Mom smiled wryly. "Goodness! Brian's here less than twenty-four hours and I'm already talking like him!" She leaned forward and pecked each of us on the cheek. "Bye, fellas. Have a good day." She strode off down the hall, her heels tapping a quick rhythm.

"Okay. Let's see your schedule," I said. "This is second period. What do you have?"

"Math. Room 220. Mr. Gordon."

"Hey, that's *my* class. Great!"

"Just a sec. I like to know what I'm getting into. What's Gordon like?"

"Like what?" I asked, starting down the hall.

"Well, take Turner, for instance. You gotta know she's a soft touch. Feed her a little compliment and she eats right out of your hand. What about Gordon?"

"Mr. Gordon? He's a nice guy, I guess. Never thought much about it."

"Tim, old boy, *think* about it. It's important." Brian loped along beside me. "To get along in this world you gotta know what makes people tick. Believe me. Now fill me in. What's Gordon like?"

"I guess you could say he's tough, but fair. Expects work on time and neat. Tests us once a week."

"Personal?"

"You mean, what do I know about his private life?"

"Right," Brian said.

I lowered my voice. "He's got a Down's syndrome kid. That's all I know."

"Down's syndrome, huh? That's a mental retard, right? Does he hang around here much?"

I shrugged. "I've seen him once or twice. Why?"

With a burst of energy, Brian took the stairs two at a time, then swung around at the landing to block my way. "What about the others?" He consulted his program. "O'Brian. Goldstein. Barone? The phys. ed. coach?"

I filled him in on what little I knew about the other teachers, including gossip I'd heard about their personal lives.

"I owe you," Brian said as we approached our math room.

"You don't owe me a thing," I said. "I haven't told you anything everyone doesn't already know."

"Never mind. I owe you." Brian placed one hand on the doorknob. "I'm gonna show you how to do what you want, stuff maybe you never dared, without Aunt Barbara having a clue."

A thrill of uneasy excitement rushed through me. What did he mean? Smiling, Brian opened the door to our math room and held it for me to go by.

● ● ●

At lunchtime, as soon as Brian sat down with his tray, even before I had a chance to introduce him, he had all my friends in stitches. "What *is* this?" he asked. He held the plate up to his nose and crossed his eyes. He held the plate at arm's length, mouth drawn into a sour line. "What *is* this? Deviled fish brains? Refried cat? Shit?"

I don't know anyone who likes cafeteria food much and Brian's reaction reminded us. He put on such a good act that everyone wanted to know where he came from and why, and by the time lunch period ended, he belonged. Maybe not to the group of his choice, but to a group—my group, my friends.

My friends are like me—kind of normal—average. We don't do drugs. Maybe we'll have a beer now and then, but nobody gets sloshed. We don't party much and we usually hang out in a group—only now some of the guys are beginning to date. Our biggest complaint is the pressure we get for good grades because our parents expect us to get into the best colleges. We're into tennis, basketball, and volleyball. Football we leave to the jocks. Compared to a lot of teenagers—we're angels.

"*Vanilla,*" Brian said about my friends as we left the cafeteria on the way to our fifth period classes. "White bread."

In other words, boring. Like me. He really pissed me off. What a hypocrite! "If you don't like my friends, go back to your own, or didn't you have any?" I asked.

"One or two." His lips smiled but his eyes didn't.

"Where were they hiding? I *sure* didn't meet any." I glared at him, wanting to add "at your parents' funeral."

He gave me a smile I couldn't read, looked at his schedule for fifth period and sailed off with *"Sayonara."*

I didn't see my cousin again until after school. I'd walked out with Gina and was waiting at the curb with her for her ride. She asked how Brian was getting along and I filled her in, without going into detail. I kept my mean thoughts to myself. I didn't want Gina to say again that I was jealous of Brian.

The buses filled and pulled out, leaving the usual stench. The parking lot was emptying of motorcycles and cars. And along came Brian, loaded down with new books.

"Gina, right?" he said. "Prettier than your picture."

Gina blushed. "Brian?"

"The same. I've been watching you two. You look so serious. What's cuz been doing—telling you about me?"

"He says you've got a bit of the devil in you. Is that true?" Gina glanced at me and smiled.

I squirmed, not happy with the easy familiarity between Brian and my girlfriend.

"A bit of the devil? Why, Tim! You flatter me!" Brian shifted his load of books. "I'll try to live up to my reputation. Now, where's that locker you were supposed to show me. I want to get rid of these."

"All of them? Don't you have homework?"

He rolled his eyes at Gina as if to say—what a jerk! "I'll borrow *your* books if I have to. Okay?"

"Sure, okay!"

"You two go ahead," Gina said. "Here comes my ride. See you, Tim. Nice meeting you, Brian." Gina slipped between parked cars and waved down the Volvo with her mom inside.

"Let's go." I strode back to the main building, not even trying to hide my anger.

Brian caught up. "Hey, didn't mean to embarrass you back there, but honestly, Tim, you sounded just like someone's mom. I'm a big boy now. I don't need you telling me to bring home my books!"

"I was only trying to save you trouble. At our house you can't get away with a thing. There are rules about homework and when to go to bed and stuff like that. If you come home without books, Mom's gonna know and Dad's gonna want to know why." I headed up the stairs to the second floor.

"Thanks for the warning, but don't worry. I

never had trouble handling my parents, and I won't with yours. It's an art."

"Fine. It's your life!" If *he* didn't worry what my parents might think, why should I? I walked ahead in a bit of a sulk while Brian sailed along like he had everything under control. Aunt Linda and Uncle Pete must have trusted him a lot to give him so much freedom. Maybe he *could* teach me a thing or two.

I glanced at the door as we passed room 220, our math class. Looking through the glass window was Mr. Gordon's son, a big hulk of a fourteen-year-old with strange looking eyes. He tapped on the glass and waved to us.

Brian waved back. "I bet kids like that can get into lots of trouble. They don't know any better."

"Nah," I said. "Down's syndrome kids are supposed to be happy and good-natured."

"Yeah?"

"Yeah." I had a feeling Brian didn't believe me, not only that, but that he'd just gotten a terrific idea.

5

Mom fingered her cheek. "The Novocain hasn't worn off yet. It feels so swollen." She'd been lying down when we got home from school but came into the kitchen to see that we had something to eat. I used to get my own snacks when she worked, but now that she's home all the time she thinks that's *her* job.

"You just sit down, Aunt Barbara," Brian said when Mom started to the fridge. He pulled out a chair for her. "We'll help ourselves. Can I get you anything? Ice water, maybe? It might help with the swelling."

Brian scores again. Why hadn't I thought to help Mom?

"Oh, thank you, Brian!" Mom sat and leaned her elbows on the table. "You're so considerate, but I don't need a thing. So, tell me—how was school?"

I brought the milk container to the table with

a jar of cookies and went after glasses. Brian, meanwhile, settled himself in the chair opposite Mom and leaned toward her. He told about his different classes. He praised my friends as if he'd never said a mean word about them. He raved about how helpful I'd been.

I poured the milk and took a chair. Mom didn't even notice me; she was intent on listening to my cousin.

Brian gobbled cookies. He told Mom she should be a decorator, she did such a great job on my—*our* room—even loved those ugly orange bedspreads I loathed. He gobbled more cookies and said he'd always longed for a brother to share with and now he had one.

Mom took in Brian's praise like a dry sponge takes in water. I watched and sipped my milk, listened and nibbled my cookie and *fumed*. He sure knew how to lay on the charm. And what about *my* day? When would Brian shut up and give *me* a chance?

Mom and I had gotten into a nice routine sitting in the kitchen after school. Usually we'd talk about all kinds of things, and sometimes we'd get into really deep stuff, like when we were studying Vietnam in school. I'd learned things about Mom I never knew. She'd marched against the war and lost two really good friends to it. With Brian hogging Mom's attention I'd never get to have conversations like that with Mom again.

Cookie skipped into the room before I could

get a word in edgewise and went directly to Brian. "Look! Look what I did at school, Brian! Just for you!" She laid a big drawing on the table in front of him, ignoring me and Mom. It appeared to be a picture of a house with five stick figures standing in a row in front.

"This is our house," Cookie explained. "And this is Mommy. And Daddy. And Tim. And me. And this is *Brian*!" she added triumphantly.

A small smile flickered across Brian's face. Cookie had drawn him almost twice as big as anyone else.

"That's wonderful, Caroline!" Brian announced, making her feel grown up by not using her nickname. "You're a terrific artist. May I keep this?"

Cookie's eyes widened. Speechless, she nodded.

Mom checked her watch. "Better get going. I promised Mr. Brady at the kennel that we'd pick up Plato before five."

Brian jumped up to pull the chair back for Mom. "I'll be glad to drive, Aunt Barbara, if you're not up to it. Mom used to let me drive all the time."

"She did?" I asked, throwing Mom an accusing look.

"But Brian! How is that possible? You're under age." Mom dug around in her purse. "Now where did I put my car keys?"

"It's true, though!" Brian spoke with great sincerity. "I look older than fifteen and Mom let me take the car lots of times to pick up groceries and things, when she was busy."

"Did you hear that, Mom?" I cried, opening the door to the garage. "Aunt Linda let—"

"I heard." Mom cut me short. "No one in this house drives a car without a license. Sorry, Brian. You'll be sixteen before you know it. Be patient. Cookie, zip your jacket. Tim, bring the leash." Distracted, Mom strode by me to her car.

Brady's Kennels, where we sometimes board Plato, is about a twenty-minute drive from home. It's down a dirt road behind a riding stable. You can see the horses being exercised in the paddocks as you drive by. The air is full of dust and horse smells and the trees look almost black from lack of water.

The kennels consist of two long, low buildings where the animals are kept and a house where Mr. Brady and his family live. His kids were in the yard, one swinging idly from a tree tire, the other digging in the dirt.

The dogs began barking as soon as Mom parked. "I hear Plato!" I said, leaping out of the car. "Come on. He knows we're here!" I headed for the office, which led through to the kennels, with Brian close behind.

Mr. Brady's a big man with a beard and long

hair tied behind in a ponytail. He looks tough, but he's a pussycat around animals. I introduced Brian, then asked, "Plato ready?"

"Sure is. Sensed you coming about ten minutes ago. That tail started wagging; near wagged the whole dog." Mom and Cookie came into the office. "Afternoon, ma'am. Plato's ready, all bathed and brushed and wantin' to go home. You just wait here and I'll bring him out."

"Can we go, too?" I asked.

Mr. Brady lifted a handful of keys from a hook on the wall. "Sure, come right along." He led me and Brian through the office to the kennels, leaving Mom and Cookie talking to Mrs. Brady.

I heard Plato's bark far down at the end and hurried toward it, past cages filled with dogs. Some wagged their tails, gripping the chain link with their forepaws, whining to be let out. Some lay uncaring on the floor of their cages. Some barked their hearts out at us.

Brian jumped away as a German shepherd bared its teeth and snarled when we passed.

"Not to worry, son. He's mean, but safe behind bars," Brady said.

I glanced back and saw Brian's face had paled and perspiration showed above his lip. "No dog scares *me*," he said.

When I reached his kennel, Plato went crazy. He clawed at the fence, whining with joy, tail wagging furiously. I could hardly wait for Brady to unlock the door.

"Hey, Plato!" I wrapped my arms around my dog and snapped the leash onto his collar. "How ya doin' boy? Miss me? Miss me, huh?" I roughed Plato's neck fur and kissed his nose. He rested his paws on my shoulders and licked my face.

"So—this is Plato!" Brian put a hand on Plato's head.

Plato swung around, growled viciously, and bared his teeth. Before I could stop him he sank his teeth into Brian's hand.

Brian jumped back, thrust his bleeding hand to his mouth, and howled, "Damn dog! He bit me!"

I yanked at Plato's leash, trying to keep him off Brian. I couldn't believe it. In the seven years we'd had Plato he hadn't once hurt anyone. "What did you do to him? He *never* bites!" I cried.

"Yeah? Well, look at this!" Blood seeped from teeth marks on the fleshy part of his palm. Brian sucked at it, eyes narrow and dark. "That dog's vicious!"

"He is not!" I stroked Plato, trying to calm him. "It's your fault. You should have known. You don't touch a strange dog when he's so excited!"

"That dog's mean! You should put him away!" There was something so cold, so ominous in his tone that I stepped back.

"Let me see that." Mr. Brady took Brian's hand. "It's not so bad. Just a nip. Come inside.

We'll clean it up and you'll be good as new in no time."

Brian and Mr. Brady started back to the office. I followed, pulled along by Plato and seething with resentment. They say dogs "know" about people. Maybe Plato sensed something about Brian the rest of us didn't.

"I'm sorry Plato hurt you, dear," Mom said, after Brady had patched Brian up. "It's just not like him. Maybe he thought you were trying to hurt Tim. I can't think of any other reason. But I promise you. Give that dog one hour and you'll adore him as much as we do."

"Yeah, sure," Brian agreed, all smiles for Mom. "But just for a while I'll keep my distance."

You do that, I said silently.

6

On Sunday afternoon Mom and Dad took Cookie to the zoo.

"You guys want to come along?" Dad asked while Mom transferred stuff from her big purse to a fanny pack.

"No, thanks. I've got a book report due," I said.

"I'll just stick around and keep Tim company," Brian added. "Besides, I've got homework, and I want to write Grandma."

Dad's face brightened. "Isn't that nice? Hearing from you will mean a lot to her."

"No big deal. She *is* my grandmother."

"How about you dropping a note, too, Tim?" Mom said.

I made a face. Writing anything is always a chore for me and letters are the worst. Why should Grandma want to read about what goes on at school? In fact, why should Brian want to write Grandma if he was so sure she didn't like him?

Mom hung a sweater around her shoulders and took Cookie's hand. "Okay, guys. We're on our way. We'll bring back pizza for dinner, so save your appetites."

As soon as they left Brian plinked around at the piano and I went upstairs to get my book. We'd been assigned *The Chocolate War* and I'd only gotten halfway through. I took it out to the balcony, sat down, tilted my chair back and rested my feet on the balcony rail. Before long I forgot everything except what was happening to Jerry Renault.

An hour later Brian's voice yanked me back from the terrible fight in the school stadium. "Hey, Tim! Come down. Let's have some fun!" he called. I held my place with a finger and peered over the rail. Brian squinted up at me, one hand shading his eyes. Plato sat beside him, wagging his tail.

"In a minute! Gotta finish this!" I held up the book for him to see.

"Forget it. I'll tell you how it ends. Saw the video."

"I've only got another twenty pages; I'm at the exciting part!"

"Oh, man! You're such a *nerd*! Come down *now* or you'll be sorry!"

I hesitated, challenged by his tone. I really wanted to finish the book, but all week long he'd made me feel like a twelve-year-old with zits. "All right!" I called. "I'm coming."

"Good!" He started toward the house. "I've got a surprise you're just gonna *love*!"

I dropped my book and raced down the stairs. Brian had been saying he'd show me a thing or two about getting what I wanted without my parents coming down on me. Was that the surprise?

"Well, that didn't take long, did it?" Brian said, waiting for me at the foot of the stairs. He held a bunch of keys by two fingers, swinging them back and forth so they jangled. "See this? The mice will play while the cat's away—"

"Hey! Those are Mom's keys!"

He grinned, swung around, and headed for the kitchen.

"Where'd you get them?" I hurried after him. "You took them from Mom's purse, didn't you!"

"Tch-tch-tch." Brian threw me a look of utter disgust. "Maybe I did and maybe I didn't. Whatever. But now *we* have them, and guess what?" He opened the door to the garage and pressed the button to raise the garage door. "What is it you're so hot to do that Momma won't allow until you're a 'big' boy?"

Heat rushed to my face at his insulting words and tone. But a sudden and exhilarating excitement rushed to my heart.

He smiled. "You guessed it. we're going for a joy ride and guess who'll be in the driver's seat?"

My mouth went dry and my pulse hammered

in my ears as I followed him. "Hey, but I don't have a license yet! What if Mom finds out?"

Brian jangled the keys. "There you go again. Who's gonna tell? Come on; I'll give you your first lesson."

I glanced hungrily at the silver Volvo in the garage, remembering the hundreds of times I'd sat beside Mom, wanting to be at the wheel. From the time I was big enough to fit in a car seat, consciously or unconsciously I'd recorded everything she ever did: how she backed the car out, checked the road before pulling into the street, the distance she kept from vehicles in front, how she took corners. . . . Everything. And always, always, I pictured myself where she sat, behind that wheel—doing just what she did. It looked so easy. I knew, without ever having driven, everything I'd have to do.

I licked my lips, unable to take my eyes from the car. I could feel that wheel under my fingers, sense my foot on the gas pedal. The joy, the power! I knew I could do it; I could drive as well as Mom—now!

"C'mon, c'mon. C'mon. . . ." Brian coaxed, beckoning with a finger. He opened the door on the driver's side and backed away. He cocked his head, smiled, and shook the car keys at me again. "Let's go, Tim! Haven't got all day!"

I felt like a sleepwalker, a magnet drawn to iron. I climbed into the car, gripped the steering wheel with both hands, and closed my eyes. The smell of leather and gasoline made me dizzy with power. I set back the seat, repositioned the mirror, and grinned at Brian.

"Yeah!" He chuckled. "Let's go have us some fun!" He let out a wild yell and plunged the key into the ignition.

My palms were wet. My legs shook. I turned the key and listened to the sweet roar of the engine, then let out the brake. Slowly, slowly, braking jerkily, I backed down the driveway like a drunken sailor. When I reached the curb I was soaked with perspiration. "Where ya wanna go, man?" I asked, throwing Brian a scared grin.

Brian folded his arms over his chest. "It's *your* show, cuz. I'm just here for the ride!"

I lurched into the road, braked, then slowly, slowly, brought the car around and started down the block.

"Yahoo!" I yelled, glancing happily at Brian. In the second my eyes left the road a kid on a skateboard zoomed out of a driveway. I saw him just as he wheeled right in front of us. "Watch it!" I screamed, jamming my foot on the brake pedal just in time. "Oh, man. I nearly killed him!" I leaned on the steering wheel, soaking wet and out of breath.

"No way! You didn't even come close, and anyway, it was his fault." Brian pulled a pack of cigarettes from his jacket and casually lit one. "Now, get this crate moving."

"Maybe we should go back."

"Don't be a wimp! Put your foot on the gas and *go*! You were doing great. There's not even any traffic. Go!"

I gripped the steering wheel with both hands, so hard my knuckles turned white. Brian would lose all respect for me if I quit now. *I'd* lose all respect for me. All the times I'd begged, nagged, bargained for a chance to drive and been turned down. Here I was behind the wheel at last.

I pressed lightly on the gas pedal and eased down the block at five miles an hour. I didn't look right or left, didn't dare blink. Just stared straight ahead and in my rearview mirror. At each corner I slowed or stopped, anxious about other cars. A mile or two along and I began to get the hang of it—the steering, how much pressure I needed on the gas pedal. I turned corners and stopped at traffic lights. The tension in my jaw eased. I grinned at Brian. "Hey, this is great!"

"Sure. See all the things you've missed? Now, pick up the speed or I'm going to have to take over. You're driving like an old lady." Brian puffed on his cigarette, closed his eyes, and leaned back. "Since we're going to be brothers, tell me, Tim—tell me one thing about yourself no one else knows."

I licked my lips, concentrating so completely on driving that without thinking I blurted out what no one except my parents knew about me. It seemed right to share the confidence if we were to be real friends and brothers. "I can't stand being cooped up in small spaces, like elevators, even airplanes. Like when we flew East? I had to take a tranquilizer or I'd have been running down the aisle screaming 'Let me out!' "

Brian smiled as if he understood so I was glad I'd told him.

"What about you?" I asked. "What's one thing about you that no one else knows?"

Brian tossed his cigarette out the window. Instead of answering my question, he said, "Take us by the school. Wake me when we get there." He yawned, lowered his seat, and crossed his arms as if going to sleep.

"Hey, you didn't answer. What's one thing about you no one else knows?"

"You wouldn't believe me."

"Try!"

He smiled, eyes closed. "I 'offed' my parents."

"Oh, sure!" I swerved, nearly hitting a car as I took my eyes from the road for an instant. "Come on; be serious," I chided.

"I am serious." He opened one eye, studied me, and added, "Sure, I'm kidding! You believe everything."

"Phew!" I took a deep breath. "For a minute there, you really had me."

"Yeah. Tell me, if you thought I had, what would you do?"

I stopped at a red light and looked at him. He was staring straight ahead. "But you didn't. You couldn't."

A funny smile lit his face. "That's right."

A chill went through me for a fleeting second and then Brian opened the glove compartment and pulled out a map. "How about we go downtown. I haven't been there yet."

Downtown meant taking the freeway. I wasn't ready for that. "Let's not. I've had enough. Let's head home."

Brian checked his watch. "Your folks won't be home for another hour, at least. Let's go see Gina."

I swerved, almost grazing a parked car. Gina knew I wasn't allowed to drive. "Nah," I lied. "She won't be home."

"Okay, so what else can we do?" He thought a moment then said, "Tell you what. Pull over and let me take 'er. I wanna see what this baby can do."

I scraped the front right tire against the curb as I brought the car to a stop. I was sweaty and tense, but from excitement, not fear. Lots of times I didn't like Brian, but I had to respect him for having guts, for risking and testing limits I never dared. I could drive; I always knew I could, and he helped me prove it!

Brian came around the car to my side. "My turn, move over."

I scooted into the seat he'd just vacated. Brian released the brake. "As they say about Greyhound, Just leave the driving to us. Here we go!"

Without checking the rearview mirror, he stepped on the gas and zoomed off down the road.

Man, he could drive! He played that car like a stunt driver. One minute he'd cruise along within the speed limit, whistling "Yankee Doodle." The next he'd floor the gas pedal, then make a turn so fast the tires squealed and we swerved all over the road. He turned on the radio and tapped one hand on the steering wheel, drumming in time to the music.

"Yahoo!" I yelled, slapping my knee to the music.

"Watch this!" Brian winked at me, passed three or four cars, went through a yellow light, then shot ahead. I heard the screech of metal scraping metal and swung around.

"Stop! Brian, stop! You hit that car back there!"

"Keep your shirt on. Nobody saw it, so we're outta here."

"What about Mom's car? Stop and let's look!"

"Shut up!" He raced down the block, hung a left, and soon swung onto the freeway ramp, doing sixty.

I gripped the sides of the seat, eyes fixed on the road and houses flashing by. We should have stopped, should have checked to see what damage we'd done, left a note on the car's windshield with our phone number. But if we had, we'd be in real trouble! "Where are we going?"

Brian ignored me, leaned over the wheel, moved from lane to lane without signaling, picked up speed.

I felt sick. Mom and Dad would have a fit. With the damaged door, there was no way to hide taking the car out. The speedometer rose to seventy. "Damn it, Brian!" I shouted. "Slow down! What if the cops stop us?"

Brian chuckled, not at all worried.

I braked the floor with my feet and pressed my hands against the seat. We whizzed by cars and trees and houses.

"Brian!" I yelled, just as he drifted over the line and nearly hit the guard rail. "Oh, man!" I covered my face with my hands.

"Got your adrenaline going, didn't I, cuz? Cool it. I'll get you home all right, safe and sound. Shoot! *Cops!*" He slowed quickly to the legal speed, eyes darting from the road to the rearview mirror. When he could, he drifted to the slower lane.

My heart thumped a crazy wild beat. What if they were after us because of the accident? We had no license, were under age, and driving too fast. I held my breath, waiting, expecting the scream of the siren, the flash of red lights, the confrontation. The police car pulled alongside, kept pace with our fifty-five miles. Brian nodded at the officer beside the driver. Then, the car sped off, leaving us both behind.

"*Sayonara!*" Brian said softly. "Lucky I saw them in time." He winked at me. "Told you we'd have fun. Count this as a down payment. Now we'll head home. Wouldn't want to get back after the folks."

I chewed on my lip and picked at my nails all the way home. It wasn't right, what we'd done, none of it, from the moment we took Mom's car. There had to be scratches. How could we explain them? And what about the other car? I was trying to work out in my head how to tell my folks, how to pay back what we'd damaged. Brian, on the other hand, whistled as he drove, like none of this bothered him at all.

As soon as we pulled into the garage I jumped out of the car to examine the door. "Look at this!" There were three horizontal scratches on the passenger door side.

Brian come around the car. "No problem."

"What do you mean, no problem? How can we explain this?"

"Ever hear of touch-up paint?" He opened the glove compartment and held up a small bottle.

"And the other car?"

"They must have insurance."

"You don't have much of a conscience, do you?" I asked, sarcastically.

He raised one eyebrow and smiled. "Tim, cuz, you've been too sheltered. Real guys do things like this all the time."

How easily Brian could make me feel like a wimp.

"Now, pay attention," he went on while

applying paint over the scratches. "If you ever take the car out yourself, don't forget to set the seat forward again and readjust the mirror. Close the garage door, and put the keys back. Especially don't forget the keys. Got it, cuz?"

Trembling with rage and uncertainty, I stood by while he recapped the paint bottle and regarded his work. "Not bad. Probably won't even notice it. And if they do—I'll think of something. Now, let's get something to eat."

In the kitchen Brian grabbed an apple. "This is how your book ends." He chewed thoughtfully for a moment, then said, "Jerry's beaten to within an inch of his life. He's laying there in the ring, bleeding, in agony, and says, 'I shoulda sold the chocolates.' See? He finally got it: *People are rotten*." He winked, but there was no warmth or humor in his eyes. "Now *you* owe me. *Sayonara*. Gotta write that letter to Grandma, now."

7

A half hour later I heard the garage door lift and then voices. "We're home!" Mom called from downstairs. "Pizza in five minutes!"

My mouth went dry and my legs got weak. How could I face Mom and Dad?

Brian yawned, got up, and stretched. "Coming? Don't want that pizza getting cold."

I'd tried to concentrate on the book report while Brian sat on his bed writing Grandma, but I hadn't written a word. Whenever I let myself relive the minutes behind the wheel, the awful screech when we grazed the parked car, the police coming up from behind and then pacing us, I sprouted goose bumps. And a million questions raced through my head. Did Brian get away with this kind of thing all the time? Didn't he feel even a little guilty? Was I making too much of what he called "a little prank"?

Brian dropped his pad on the bed and went

to the mirror to comb his hair. Cool as you please, as if he'd been home all afternoon doing homework. Why couldn't I be like that? Why did I feel so scared to face my family?

"Listen, cuz," Brian said, meeting my eyes in the mirror. "Chill out. The way you're acting, you'd think you just robbed Fort Knox. Get real, man. Kids do that kind of thing all the time. You know who should feel bad? Your folks, that's who!"

My folks feel guilty? How did he figure that?

He waved his comb in the air. "You're fifteen, man! You've always been responsible. Your folks know you could drive, but they're sticklers for dumb rules. They just don't want you to grow up!"

"It's not that; it's the law."

"Dumb law. Now, if you're worried about those scratches, don't. They'll probably not even notice, and if they do I'll just say it must have happened when your mom parked when shopping, and that I saw it and touched it up with paint. No big deal. I'll come out a hero."

"Another lie!"

Brian threw me a pained expression. "Chill out, and wipe that guilty look off your face. Let's go."

Mom was setting the table when we reached the family room. I headed for the fridge to put out the drinks so I wouldn't have to look at her.

"How'd you guys make out? Get your work

done?" Mom asked, dropping napkins at each setting. "*We* had a lovely afternoon. The weather was perfect. The zoo wasn't too crowded. Cookie loved it. Did you two get outdoors a bit, I hope?"

Brian brought glasses to the table. "We played with Plato for a while," he said.

"Get your letter written?" Mom smiled at him as she went for the pizza box.

"Most of it."

Dad came in from the garage. I'd heard him rolling the garbage cans out to the curb for pickup Monday. He went to the sink to wash. "I think there's something wrong with the Volvo," he said.

A spike of alarm raced down my arms and I darted a glance at Brian. He whistled softly as he brought plates to the table. I held my breath and watched Mom.

"What kind of trouble? I drove it yesterday and it seemed fine." Mom motioned for us to sit and began dishing out wedges of pizza. "I just had it in for its twenty-thousand-mile checkup. What could be wrong? Cookie!" she called. "It's time!"

"It's hot." Dad wiped his hands and came to the table. "I touched the hood as I went by. If it hasn't been driven since yesterday, it shouldn't be *hot*."

I tried not to choke on my pizza.

"Maybe it's a short," Brian offered. "We once had that problem. Nearly had a fire."

"Don't think so." Dad's gaze made me squirm.

"That *is* weird." Brian's forehead wrinkled in concern. "Maybe you should check it again later. If it hasn't cooled off, get triple A to tow it to a garage." Without a pause he changed the subject. "This pizza's fantastic, Aunt Barbara. Dad used to bring pizza home when Mom worked late, but it was never this good!"

"I'm glad you like it. Have some more." Mom lifted another wedge onto Brian's plate. "And Brian, dear. I'm so glad you can talk about your parents now. It's important that you do. We've worried that you're bottling up your grief and that's not healthy."

"I'll remember that." Brian bent his head so I couldn't tell what he thought or felt.

Dad knew! I was sure of it. What other explanation could there be for the car being hot? And he was choosing not to make an issue of it because of Brian! I escaped to our room as soon as dinner ended, hoping Brian would come up so we could talk about it. But he stayed downstairs watching *60 Minutes* with Mom and Dad.

Anxious, guilty, angry, I wandered around the room listening for his footsteps, hearing only the voices of TV. I picked up books and laid them down. I ran a finger over the sleek back of a wooden duck I'd carved last year. When I reached Brian's bed I saw the yellow pad on his spread. Usually, he put everything away with almost military neatness. Had he left the pad there deliberately? What had he written Grandma, I wondered. Did he say anything about me, about our family?

Impulsively, I picked up the pad. With an ear to footsteps and one eye on the door, I dropped onto my bed and opened it. "Dear Grandma," the first page read. And that was all. It was as if he couldn't get past the greeting, couldn't figure out what to say.

I turned to the next page. On this one Brian had drawn three tombstones. Two of them had his parents' initials on them. The third was very black and *Martha*—Grandma's first name—had been scratched through the black. Poor guy, I thought. Here was the grief Mom thought he was holding in—spread all over the page. He even worried that Grandma, his last link with home, might die.

I turned to the next page. This one was bordered in black. Crowded all over in the most intricate detail were witches and devils and evil looking animals, their mouths spewing slime and putrefaction. Really gross, the kind of thing you see in horror comics. I turned the page around and tried to make out some scribbles he'd drawn in one corner. At first it looked only like a lot of X's. Then, under the X's I could make out what seemed like two boxes, almost the shape of coffins. Inside, under the heavy load of X's, I could barely see some letters. I held the paper up to the light and squinted. Was that *T.A.* and *C.A.*? I pulled at the neck of my shirt in sudden panic. *T.A.* and *C.A.*! Cookie's and my initials!

What did it mean? I threw the pad down, as if it had sprouted worms, all worry about Dad and his suspicions forgotten. While I'd been sitting at my desk working on the report, Brian had been only feet away—thinking what? Drawing these bizarre things! Did his parents' deaths make him afraid everyone else might die? I had a second, much more scary, thought. *Did he want me and Cookie dead?*

"You should have stayed downstairs and watched TV with us," Brian said, coming into the room. "There was a real neat segment about animals. They showed some of the experiments they do on dogs!" He glanced at his bed and put two and two together. "Been spying on me?"

I backed away. "You sure draw weird stuff. You should see a shrink."

"Don't *ever* say that!" His eyes turned black and his tone sent a chill through me.

"I thought you were writing Grandma. You never even got started. That notebook is full of tombstones. You've even drawn caskets with my initials and Cookie's. Gives me the shivers. Planning to 'off' us like you said you did your parents?"

"That's not funny."

"No it's not. You scare me."

"Good. I figured I could." Brian dropped onto

his bed and smiled at me. "I knew if I left my pad around you couldn't resist taking a peek. I drew that stuff on purpose, just to get a little rise out of you. And it worked." He raised that one eyebrow again in a quizzical glance that made me feel dumb. He'd set me up, just for the effect.

"But you said you'd written Grandma," I returned, weakly.

"Wrote it at school. I'll show you tomorrow if you want."

He'd won again, turned my suspicion into doubt. "Well, what about Dad? He *knows* we took the car out. He's no dummy!"

Brian picked up his pad and slid it under some clothes in a dresser drawer. "You worry too much, Tim. Your dad didn't accuse you, did he? Just watch. He'll check the car again, find it's cold, and that'll be the end of it."

I opened my mouth, then shut it. He was probably right. Still, I felt uneasy about everything connected with Brian. He lied so easily and justified it so well.

"Chill out, Tim. All we did was have some fun. Nothing to get upset about." He opened the doors to the balcony and stretched, breathing the night air deeply. Then, he leaned over the railing. "Plato! Here, dog! Here, Plato!" he called.

I joined him at the balcony. Plato, on the lawn below, yipped with joy, jumping as high as he could, trying to get to us. "Let's take him for a walk. He's always locked in the yard, poor dog. Let's show him a little of the outside world!" Brian said. "Come on, brother, just you and me."

If I had any doubts, his calling me 'brother' erased them.

"We're taking Plato for a walk," I told Mom a few minutes later, picking up the leash that hangs near the garage door.

"Don't be too late. School tomorrow!"

"Lesson number one." Brian held the leash as Plato pulled us down the block. "Don't feel you've gotta tell your parents where you're going or why every time you leave the house."

I nodded. From the time I was a kid Mom always expected to know my whereabouts, just as I got to know where she'd be at any given time. But Brian was right. At fifteen you shouldn't have to account for your every move.

"Since we're going to be buddies," Brian added, accepting my nod for agreement, "let's set some rules."

Plato sniffed around a tree. Brian yanked him on.

"Rule one. *You* cover for me and *I* cover for you."

"Cover for what?"

"For anything."

I dug my hands into my pockets against a sudden chill. "What kind of things?"

Brian stopped under a tree for Plato to relieve himself. In the dark I couldn't read his face.

"Like, for instance, let's say some night I'm supposed to be at the library and I'd rather be somewhere else."

"Like, where?"

"I don't know! Just taking a walk, maybe. Getting away from people to think."

"Yeah, so?"

"So if anyone asks, you cover for me, that's all. And vice versa. Let's say you decide some night to skip over to Gina's or wherever, when you're supposed to be home studying. You get the idea. See no evil, speak no evil, hear no evil. Deal?"

Why not? I wasn't about to commit any crimes when I went where I wasn't supposed to be, right? A few secrets from my parents lent a kind of excitement to what would probably be pretty innocent. "Deal," I said.

He nodded. "Rule two. You do your thing and I do mine, no questions asked. Deal?"

That seemed a little strange. If we were buddies, wouldn't we want to talk about what we did? Still, maybe that would come. "Okay, deal."

Brian and I slapped hands to bind the agreement and we walked on.

"Now tell me about your neighbors," he said. "Like, who lives in this house, and what are they like? Do they both work? Any kids? Do the cats yowl on the fence like that every night?"

I told him all I knew and asked, "Why do you want to know all that boring stuff?"

We headed back to the house with Plato still tugging at the leash. "I'm just a curious fella," Brian said. "If you moved to a strange place, wouldn't you be?"

8

"Look." Brian held up a stamped, addressed envelope thick enough to hold several folded sheets. We were at school. "I told you I'd written. Here's that letter to Grandma."

"I didn't doubt you," I lied.

"Sure you did." He popped the envelope back in his notebook before I could see it up close. "Want to fool around this afternoon?"

"Doing what?" A jolt of fear and excitement rushed through me.

"I'll think of something." He sauntered off to his next class, calling over his shoulder, "*Sayonara!*"

I nibbled the skin around my thumb, watching him disappear in the crowd of students. I'd relived yesterday's escapade a dozen times, and each time felt the same mix of guilt and thrill. Still, everything had worked out okay and Brian was calling me "brother." I didn't *have* to go along with his plans. Why not at least see what he was up to?

"So, where are you going?" Mom asked as we left the house later.

"Out," Brian said.

She didn't look pleased. "When will you be back?"

"Later." Brian lifted a banana from the fruit bowl and opened the door. Cool. It took real talent—answering questions without giving a thing away.

"So, where *are* we going?" I asked.

"First, to the General Store."

"What for?"

"Why don't you just wait and see?" He rolled his eyes toward heaven.

I strode beside him, almost biting my tongue to keep from asking more questions. Brian whistled tunelessly, his attention on a neighbor and her dog, a kid playing with his cat, a United Parcel truck parked in front of a house. I might as well have been alone for all the interest he showed in me.

"Hey, cuz," I said finally, using the name he calls me. "What kind of things did you do back East? Did you hang around with friends a lot?"

"Not much. I prefer my own company most of the time." He didn't look at me.

"But what do you do alone? You don't read much, or listen to music. What do you do when you go out?"

"Did you forget rule two already? You do your thing and I do mine, no questions asked?"

"Come on. Why so mysterious? What can you do that you wouldn't want me to know about?"

"We turn here," he said, not answering. "Yes, there's the General Store. Now this is what you do. You forget about me and go inside and buy something at the counter. Anything. Gum. *Mad* magazine. Whatever. Take your time choosing. Got money?"

"Yeah. But why? Where will you be?"

"Just poking around. Looking for something we need."

"What?"

"You'll see."

A woman came out of the store, followed by two little girls carrying helium balloons.

"Boy—some fun—shopping in the General Store," I muttered as I went inside.

Brian gave me a little push.

I went directly to the counter near the front door where the lady who owns the store stood beside the cash register. Brian wandered down the middle aisle toward the back.

"May I help you?" the lady asked.

"No, thanks, just looking." I pretended to examine the straw hats on a rack near the counter. They were the kind people wear at the beach to protect against the sun. I adjusted the mirror, pretending to examine the hat, but checking out

Brian at the rear of the store. His back was to me so I couldn't tell what he was doing.

"That looks very nice on you," the owner said, coming out from behind the counter. "Young man?" she called out to Brian, "May I help you find something?"

"No, thanks, I'm fine!" Brian called back.

"I'll take this," I said as alarm bells went off in my head. I carried the hat to the counter and pulled out my wallet. The saleslady went behind the counter. "That's seven ninety-five, plus tax." She glanced uneasily toward the back of the shop. How long could I divert her?

"Ready, Tim?" I jumped when Brian tapped my shoulder a moment later.

"Ready!" I swung about, ready to flee.

"Don't forget your hat!" the woman said, and to Brian, "Find what you wanted?"

Brian smiled charmingly. "No. Maybe next time."

"Well, come again," she called as the door closed behind us with a jingling bell.

"Whooosh!" I exclaimed, expecting her to come running after us to frisk Brian and find whatever it was he took. When we'd gotten far enough away I turned on him. "What was that all about? What'd you take?"

"What'd you pay for that hat?"

"Seven ninety-five. You swiped something, right?"

"Highway robbery. The hat's worth half that,

so we're even." He pulled two cans of spray paint from under his jacket. One green, one red.

"Spray paint!" I cried. "You risked getting in trouble for two dumb cans of paint?"

"Sometimes you're such a dork, Tim. Maybe you should go home."

"Maybe I should!" I hated when he called me a dork. I'd do anything to avoid it. So, I rationalized: He shoplifted a couple of cans of paint; big deal. He wanted to impress me, that's all, or maybe it gave him a thrill. Even I could feel the adrenaline pumping. Just like yesterday. No use getting all righteous about it. It was just a prank.

"What do you want the paint for, anyway?" I asked, changing my tone.

"We're going to paint a wall. How good an artist are you?"

My hands got sweaty. Guys like me didn't do things like that, especially in their own neighborhood.

"Now do you see why I couldn't 'buy' these cans?" Brian asked. Without waiting for my answer he said, "That woman might have remembered and they could be traced back to us."

He'd thought of everything.

"So? You a pretty good artist?" he asked again.

I swallowed an uncomfortable lump in my throat and nodded. Tim Anderson, Eagle Scout, good son, dependable friend, honest student—was about to become a vandal. Yahoo! It wasn't guilt

I felt, but anticipation, exhilaration, even—
liberation.

"We'll wait till that truck leaves," Brian said,
settling himself on a slope overlooking a new construction site. I sat on my haunches beside him.
"They always go home about this time. I've
picked up all kinds of useful stuff left behind—a
hammer, staple gun, tape measure. . . ."

After a while two men got into a pickup truck,
backed out of the drive of the nearest house, and
drove away.

"Let's go!" Brian slid down the dusty slope to
the house the men had left. I followed close behind. Painters' scaffolds still in place, the white
walls glittered in the late afternoon sun. "This
should do it. Here!" He tossed me the can of
green paint. "Let's use the scaffold. It'll be
easier."

"What if someone comes?" I looked about,
uneasily.

"No problem; we'll hear them in plenty of
time." He clicked his tongue and winked. "Let's
get started while the light's still good. Be sure to
shake the can first."

I hoisted myself onto the scaffold and turned
away from the wall. All around us were houses,
some almost completed, others still going up.
Other than a dog sniffing at a discarded fast food
carton, the area seemed deserted. Even so, knowing what I was about to do, my heart pounded
against my ribs.

I stared at the stark white wall. A huge surface, waiting for my mark. Where to begin? What to draw?

Brian worked steadily at the other end of the scaffold, stretching up as high as he could, then painting down to knee level. I sneaked a look, wondering what he was printing. He shook his can from time to time, then sprayed steadily, moving slowly along the platform.

Peace, I finally sprayed, adding a peace sign, then *Love* with a green heart as the dot on an exclamation point.

"You finished? Let's have a look," Brian called, dropping to the ground.

How tame my message would seem to him, I suddenly realized. How scornful he'd be. "One sec!" I called and quickly sprayed *Wussy,* with an unexpected thrill of wickedness. "Okay, done," I announced and jumped from the scaffold.

"Not bad," Brian announced. We stood side by side in the growing dark, examining our work. He had sprayed *Nuke the Whales!* and drawn a mushroom cloud on his section of wall.

"What's that zigzag thunderbolt thing doing under the *u*?" I asked.

"My signature. I always sign my art that way."

Always? He did this kind of thing a lot and got away with it?

"Wussy," Brian said, only noting the last

word I'd done. "Yeah. I like that." He clamped a friendly hand on my shoulder. "That should be *your* signature." He chuckled when I stiffened. "Just kidding. You're all right, Tim. You're not as soft as I thought. So, brother? Did I tell you or what? Wasn't this more fun than what you usually do? Huh?"

I heard a truck tooling down the road and stiffened. Brian heard it, too, but kept talking, one arm still around my shoulder. I wanted to run so badly I nearly wet my pants, but Brian wouldn't. No way. He'd wait till the very last second before he'd move. That was half the fun. And if I wanted his respect I'd have to wait, too.

9

The afternoon adventure had turned me silent and Brian hyper. While I relived the excitement and danger in my head, feeling guilty and ashamed, he burst with good cheer.

"Who's that nice old lady with the pooper scooper and the weimaraner I see all the time, Aunt Barbara?" he asked at dinner. "You sure have nice neighbors, Uncle Bill." He flirted with Cookie and got a laugh from Mom and Dad when he imitated my "brooding" face.

"Excuse me," I said as soon as I could, needing to escape, to sort out my feelings about our escapade. Mom and Dad hardly noticed my leaving. I couldn't figure it. Why had I gone along with shoplifting, with vandalism, just for the thrill, or just to get in good with a cousin I didn't really like and even distrusted? What a wimp! Regardless of how Brian described it, it was wrong!

"Look what *I've* got!" Brian said when he came

back to our room a while later. He waved a small, narrow box at me, sat on the side of his bed, and removed a harmonica. "Ever play one of these?"

"Yeah. Where'd *you* get it?" I'd been at my desk, doodling and thinking. I swung around and with all the sarcasm I could muster asked, "Where's that from? The General Store? Something else you swiped?"

"Tch-tch. You're feeling guilty, again. Now you should understand why I prefer to go it alone." Brian's voice went soft, sad. Eyes on me, he slid his mouth along the length of the instrument, testing it first with his lips. Then he blew, back and forth, repeating the same scale, almost hypnotically. I covered my ears and turned back to my worksheet.

Hats. All over the sheet I'd doodled hats. *Hats!*

Even before words came, my face flamed in sudden realization. "Brian!" I almost strangled on the words. "The hat! The hat from the General Store! I left it behind!"

Brian shook saliva from the harmonica and solemnly studied me. "I know."

"You know?" I squeaked, then threw my hand over my mouth, afraid Mom or Dad might hear. "You *know*?"

"I remembered while we were having dinner. Not to worry."

"You crazy? They could trace us! You said so yourself! When they see what we did and find the empty paint cans and the hat with the receipt in the bag, they'll go right to the store. That saleslady will remember us!"

Brian blew a thoughtful blast on the harmonica, not the least concerned.

"Brian! I've got to go back and get it before someone finds it!"

He patted the harmonica on the palm of one hand. "What's the worst scenario, huh?" Without waiting for my answer he said, "The worst thing can happen is that that woman knows *you*. Not *me* because I'm new here. You, because you've probably been in the store a dozen times, maybe even with your mom. So? She tells the police. So? They send someone to talk to us. Follow?"

I hugged the back of my chair, eyes glued to my cousin, ready to hear and believe anything he said.

"Okay, now let's play the scene. The fuzz come to the house. Knock knock. Who's there? Officer Cooper.

"Your parents call us in. Coop says they're investigating a crime of vandalism in the new housing project. Can we account for where we were last night?"

"So, what do *we* say? Mom and Dad know we were out late. The saleslady can identify us!"

"You have no imagination. Sure, you bought the hat. The very thing you thought your mom would like for around the pool next summer. No harm in admitting that. But remember when we were messing around in the project? Remember those two guys came after us? Those guys zoomed up the road on their Harleys? Wore black leather jackets with thunderbolts on the back?"

"*What* guys?"

"Oh, come on!" Brian blew another blast on the harmonica. "You know! The ones who said they'd run us over if we didn't split. Don't you remember? That's how you lost the hat. Dropped it when they chased us. Ran for our lives."

"That's a lie, Brian! There were no guys and you know it! And even if we could talk the police into believing a fish story like that, they'd find our prints on those cans!" I jumped up and found my jacket.

"Honest to God, Tim." He crossed his heart. "I don't lie. That's just how it happened. What's wrong with you? Don't you remember?"

Pulling on my jacket, I did a double take. He really believed what he said!

I grabbed a flashlight. "Doesn't matter. I've got to get that hat before someone finds it. I've done enough rotten stuff tonight without lying to the police right in front of my folks, too. See you later."

Brian glanced up with vague interest. "You're making a big deal out of nothing, cuz."

"Know what? Do me a favor. Don't invite me on any more of your fun-and-game escapades, okay? I'll do with a little less excitement." As I went out the door I added, *"Sayonara."*

10

Dad joined me in the garage a few weekends later while I cleaned my bike gears. He leaned against his car, crossed his arms, and watched me. Anxious at what was coming, I splashed alcohol in a pan, dropping more than I should, and tried to appear unconcerned.

"We don't get to talk much anymore, do we?" Dad asked after a while. "You avoiding me?"

"There's a lot been going on." I dipped the gears in the pan and swooshed them around a bit.

"Your mother says she misses those talks you used to have after school."

"That's okay. Brian talks with her now."

For a long moment Dad didn't speak, then he said, "It's not the same, you know. And Brian needs special attention now."

"I know." I wanted to scream, Brian-Brian! All anyone talks about is Brian! Don't I count anymore?

"Your mother says you avoid her. You come home, grab something to eat, and off you go to your room. Says you're like a boarder, the way you come and go. Want to talk about it?"

"There's nothing to say." I dried one line of gears, wiped away the grease, and hung it over a chair. In the weeks he'd been in our house Brian had dug his way under my family's skin, like a tick. I couldn't understand how my parents didn't see through him the way I did. And I couldn't enlighten them by telling about the car and the shoplifting and the vandalism. I'd only lose their respect and look like a jealous tattle, to boot. Lately I'd even found myself remembering those caskets he'd drawn with my initials and Cookie's and worrying that it meant more than Brian admitted.

"Look, Dad," I said, knowing he wanted more of an answer. "Mom and Brian like talking together so I figured I'd back off. As you say, Brian needs special attention now. Besides, I'm pretty busy with my own things."

"Like what?" Dad persisted.

I wiped my hands on a rag. "I'm nearly sixteen, Dad. Do I have to account for everything I do?"

"Of course not." Dad's eyes probed mine until I had to turn away.

"You're not jealous of him, are you, Tim? Because if you are, you shouldn't be. *You're* our son and we love you a lot."

"I know." I bent to undo the other gear so he couldn't see how red my face must be.

"Where is he, by the way? Where does he go on a Saturday like this? Has he any friends?"

"I'm not his keeper, Dad."

"You don't like him, do you?"

"The truth? No."

"Why?"

I shrugged. "We're just very different, I guess." But it was more than that. Not just the lies and pranks I didn't like, but something I couldn't quite put my finger on. An aloofness. A dishonesty of the heart, if you know what I mean. Like he didn't really feel what he tried to make you think he felt. But how could I explain that to Dad when I didn't even understand it myself?

Dad switched the subject. "Would you like help putting those gears back?"

"No, I can do it." I dipped the second gear in the alcohol pan.

He nodded and rubbed two fingers over his beard, thinking. "It's got to be an adjustment, sharing your space, your family. We thought it would be good, you having someone your age around. Be patient, Tim. Brian puts on this air of sophistication, but down deep he's a lonely, hurt young man. Do what you can to include him in your activities."

"Yeah, sure." I had no intention of getting closer to Brian. We shared a room, but rarely talked now. Even my friends didn't warm to him.

After the first days when he charmed everyone, interest in him burned out. Brian drifted away. I had no idea what he did with his time and didn't ask. He wouldn't have told me anyway.

Dad patted my shoulder and ambled back into the house. Irritated, I bent over my bike.

Later, I rode over to Gina's. Saturdays she has to help out around the house before she can go anywhere. She's one of five kids and her mom runs the family like an army. One kid's out washing windows, another's inside vacuuming. Someone's doing laundry or cleaning pet cages, or pulling weeds or caring for the baby.

I found Gina on the driveway washing the family van. "Soon as I finish this, I can go." She handed me an old towel. "Dry."

I crossed my arms and sat on the wall. "I'd rather just sit and watch you."

"Oh, yeah?" Gina threw the wet sponge at me.

I jumped up and chased her around the van, flicking my towel at her back.

Laughing, she grabbed the pail of soapy water, swung around, and faced me. "Truce?" Her dark eyes flashed with deviltry. "Truce, or you're gonna get it!" The water sloshed dangerously back and forth.

"You wouldn't!"

"One . . . two . . ." She swung the pail back and forth, gathering momentum.

I backed off, dropped my towel, held my

hands up in surrender, and cried "Truce! Truce!" Under my breath I mumbled, "I'll get you later!!"

Later, we cycled to the mall. Sometimes we'd run into friends there and hang out together. Maybe we'd get a burger and shake or some of Mrs. Field's chocolate chip cookies, or go to a movie or the skating rink.

"What's Mr. Mysterioso up to today?" Gina asked, pulling up beside me at a red light. She yanked off her ski cap and shook out her hair. "You might have invited him along."

"You're kidding. You know how uncomfortable he makes me." I had told Gina some things about Brian, but not the pranks I'd been involved in. She'd have lost all respect for me.

"Oh, come on, Tim! He lost his parents, his home, his friends, comes to a strange school full of cliques, and doesn't fit in anywhere. We're forcing him to become a loner. It's cruel," she said.

"Boo hoo. You're making me cry."

"Tim!"

The light changed and I pushed off, pedaling hard away from Gina. Mom, Dad, now my girl-friend. Every time Brian's name came up Gina stood up for him. Did she like him better than me?

I was a half block ahead of Gina, pedaling hard. I bounced off the curb into the road and kept going when suddenly I felt the wobble. I knew instantly—the front wheel was loose. Cars were coming. I gripped the handlebars and braced myself for the certain fall. I braked, skidded on a patch of dirt, dragged my feet along the ground, and held on for dear life. Just as I came to a stop the front wheel flew off and I nearly went with it.

I was okay. I grabbed my bike and ran to the nearest curb, left it and ran back to catch the wheel rolling down the street.

"Tim, are you okay? You could have been killed!" Gina cried as she pulled up beside me. "What happened?"

"The wheel came off," I said, hands shaking as I tried to fix it back on. Sweat ran down my neck and my pulse beat double time. "I worked on my bike this morning, took the wheels off to clean the gears. Maybe I forgot to lock the clamp. I can't believe I'd be so careless!"

"'Maybe the clamp's faulty."

"I don't think so."

"If you locked the clamp, and the clamp's not faulty, what else could it be?"

"I don't *know*!"

"Well ..." Gina said, hearing my irritation, "as long as you're okay. . . ."

"Yeah." Shaken, I hopped back on my bike and pushed off. "Let's go." No use ruining our day by making a big thing over what had to be my own dumb mistake. Still, I couldn't let go of the certainty that I *had* locked the clamp.

•   •   •

It was the Saturday before Thanksgiving but already the mall was decorated with Christmas wreaths and tinsel. Holiday music floated over the crowds. A huge tree stood high in the center of the mall and a Santa sat on a sleigh having his picture taken with all the little kids. We stood by, watching.

"You ought to bring Cookie here for a picture," Gina said.

I withdrew my arm from around her waist. "Brian asked her already. Mom and Dad were very impressed."

"How sweet! I told you! He's really very nice down deep. How many guys his age would be so thoughtful? He's lonely, Tim. Just think. When he was Cookie's age I bet his parents got Santa photos every year, and they're all gone, burned up in that fire. Poor Brian. There's no record of his past; it's like he never existed."

"Can we talk about someone else for a change?"

Gina hugged my arm and smiled indulgently. "Okay. Let's go see those kittens over there!" She drew me across the mall to where a small crowd had gathered. Seated on the ground with a box of frisky gray and white kittens was a ten-year-old boy.

"Aren't they darling!" Gina's face flushed with joy. "Can I hold one?" She bent and gently lifted one of the kittens from the box. She stroked it, held it against her cheek, and glowed. "Isn't he darling?"

"Yeah," I agreed, but I really prefer dogs. Cats are too independent and they scratch.

"Does he have a name?" Gina asked the boy.

"Puff, only he's a *she*," the kid said. "Want her?"

"I wish." Gina reluctantly placed the kitten back in the box. "My sister's allergic."

The boy turned his attention to others. We watched awhile longer, then wandered away to the record store and game shop and finally to the snack area. We ordered onion rings and shakes and settled at a table to decide whether to go to the movie or the roller rink. "Oh, there's Brian!" Gina exclaimed, her face lighting up. A knot grew in my stomach.

"Hi, guys!" Brian pulled up a chair, sat down, and helped himself to an onion ring. "What are you two up to?"

"Trying to decide whether to go skating or take in a movie. Want to join us?" Gina asked.

"Can't." Brian nibbled around the onion ring while holding one hand against his stomach. "Aren't you going to ask *why* I can't?"

"Why?" I asked, wondering what he was up to now.

"Because . . ." He partially unzipped his jacket and reached inside. "Of this." A small gray and white kitten with blue eyes scrambled up his chest and peered over the zipper at us. Brian grinned and petted the kitten's head with one finger.

"Puff!" Gina and I exclaimed together. Gina

scooted over a seat to sit next to Brian. "You adopted her! Oh, let me hold her!"

Brian lifted the kitten out and passed her over to Gina. "She's hungry. Pour some milkshake on the lid for her."

"I thought you didn't like cats," I said to Brian.

"Sure I do. Just not vicious ones." He studied me a moment, then frowned. "I *can* keep her, don't you think? I mean, your folks won't mind, will they? They let *you* have a dog. They can't say no to my having a cat, can they? I'd feed it and take care of it. I'd see it didn't cause trouble. Tim?"

"Sure," I said quickly. He seemed so genuinely anxious and needy. "If they give you any arguments, I'll back you up."

"Thanks!" Brian let out his breath. "Hey, look. I got this for your mom!" He reached into his back pocket and pulled out a small box. "Obsession. It's real expensive perfume. My dad always bought that for Mom."

"Wow! Look at the cost!" Gina said.

"How come the price tag's still on?" I challenged. "And where's the receipt?"

"Tim!" Gina cried, in disbelief.

Brian averted his eyes and pocketed the perfume. "That hurts, Tim. It really does. You think I'd *steal*? Come *on*!" He helped himself to another onion ring. "Let's get out of here."

11

"Why, Brian!" Mom exclaimed in a voice filled with surprise and delight. "A gift for me? But you shouldn't have!" Mom sat at her desk in the study, writing checks. Brian held out the perfume, nicely wrapped, and bowed.

"I wanted to, Aunt Barbara. You've been so kind, so good to me. I wanted to get you something special," Brian said.

Mom glowed. "You didn't have to buy me anything. Really! We love having you here with us!"

What a con man! I leaned against the doorjamb of the study, watching. How come Mom and Dad couldn't see through him?

He'd said he'd ask about the kitten after he gave Mom the present. "She won't be able to turn me down then," he explained. Puff scrabbled around in a box in the hall. I could hear her trying to get out.

"Open it, Aunt Barbara. I think you'll like it." Brian urged.

Mom slipped off the bow and then undid the wrapping, both of which I'd supplied, and withdrew the perfume. "Oh, my. How did you know? It's my favorite! And it's perfume, not cologne. It's so expensive! I can't let you. You must have saved every penny of your allowance these last two months."

"Grandma sent me money," Brian said.

"I thought you hadn't heard from her!" Mom said in surprise.

"Sure I heard. I got a letter just last week."

"But I didn't see . . "

"I went through the mail before you got home," Brian explained. "She wrote; honestly, Aunt Barbara. I wouldn't lie."

"Well, of course not!" Mom touched Brian's arm.

He crossed his arms over his chest and stepped out of reach. "Aunt Barbara? If I wanted something very badly, would you let me have it?"

I eased into the room and perched on the arm of Dad's lounge chair. Here comes the pitch, I thought.

"Oh, oh," Mom said. "If it's a car you want, then nothing doing, Brian. I told you *and* Tim. Not until you're of age, and then, maybe." She gathered up the stamped envelopes on her desk and stacked them neatly, then held the sealed perfume box to her nose, closed her eyes, and smiled.

"It's not a car I want, Aunt Barbara." Brian said, moving closer. "It's something much more important."

"Oh? What?"

"A kitten. I've always wanted one, ever since my cat died six years ago. I found one at the mall today. The cutest thing, gray and white with blue eyes. Some kid was giving it away, free. I've bought cat litter and cat food and all and I really want to keep her. May I, *please*?"

I could see Mom thinking: cat fur, scratches on the furniture, smells. But also: He's lost so much; maybe a cat will be good for him. With a catch in her voice she said, "Sure, honey. If that's what you want. But what do you think about Plato? Do cats and dogs get along?"

"All the time!" Brian said with great certainty. "It's all a matter of training. Honestly, I'll see she behaves. I won't let her be any trouble or make any mess and I'll keep her so quiet you'll never even know she's around! Thanks, Aunt Barbara. You're the greatest!" He threw his arms around Mom and gave her a quick hug.

"Let's go get Puff." Brian strode by me on his way out of the room. He winked, a satisfied grin on his face. "Let's see how Plato likes competition."

I ran after him into the hall. "Hey, wait! What's this about competition? I thought you wanted Plato and Puff to get along?"

"Just kidding." Brian plucked the kitten out

of the box and pressed it against his chest. "This is going to be fun!" He started out to the backyard. A second later he cried, "Cripes! Look what she did!" He thrust Puff out in front of him, a look of revulsion on his face. The whole front of his shirt was wet with a yellowish color. "Filthy cat!" He threw the kitten on the floor and pulled his shirt front away from his chest. "I'll fix her!"

"Take it easy, Brian. She's just a kitten and she's scared," I said.

"Yeah, sure. Peeyoo! I stink! Now I've gotta change!" He swung around. "You take over! Boy, just wait! She won't do *that* again!" He ran to the staircase and took the steps two at a time.

The kitten wouldn't come to me. She cowered under chairs and leaped on tables and scooted behind the couch. When I finally caught her I brought her to the kitchen to pour a saucer of milk. She was lapping happily at it when Cookie charged into the kitchen. "A kitty!" Her eyes widened with wonder. "Is it ours?" She darted a sticky finger out to touch Puff's head, then pulled it back. "Is it ours?"

"It's Brian's, Cookie. Her name's Puff. It's okay. You can touch; she won't hurt you. Here." I squatted in front of my sister, stroking the kitten's back until she purred. Pretty soon Cookie was holding the kitten, and then Brian came into the kitchen. He wore my Save the Earth T-shirt, which was tight across the chest for him.

"Brian, look! Kitty likes me! See?" The kitten

ran its little pink tongue across Cookie's cheek. She giggled, closed her eyes, and tilted her head back.

"Sure, Cookie. Everyone likes you." Brian lifted Puff by her neck fur. "Let's go outside. Show her to Plato." He guided Cookie out the door. "Come on, Tim; this should be interesting."

I scooted in front of Brian and walked backward. "Listen! Plato's pretty territorial. The backyard's his turf. Go easy. Let him get used to her gradually."

"Sure! You don't think I'd offer my cute little kitten to that dog of yours as a sacrifice, do you?"

"I hope not!"

"Ah, Tim. You always think the worst of me. That hurts."

What he said was true. I suspected Brian's every word and every act, even innocent acts. Maybe I was being too hard on him. After all, he was good to Cookie. People who liked little kids couldn't be all bad, right? And little kids had an uncanny sense about fakers, right? Still, I couldn't get rid of the feeling that Brian was out to make trouble. I fell in step beside him and grabbed the leash before leaving the kitchen.

Plato heard us coming and started an excited barking even before I opened the back door.

"Hey, fella!" Plato leaped up on me, paws on my shoulders, panting, tail wagging his body. "Down, boy!" I cried, laughing. His hot breath warmed my face and his tongue slobbered all over me. I clicked the leash onto his collar and pushed him off me.

"You like company, huh?" Brian asked, bending to scratch Plato's neck. "You're a social animal, huh?" He held the kitten behind his back. "Well, look at this pal I brought for you to play with!"

Suddenly, he pulled the kitten out from behind him and thrust it into Plato's face.

Plato snarled and bared his teeth, ready to bite the kitten's head off. Puff hissed and humped her back.

"Plato's gonna hurt the kitty!" Cookie screamed.

I yanked at Plato's leash, almost lifting him off the ground to keep his jaws from clamping on the kitten. "Damn you, Brian!" I yelled, "I told you to go slow! Get that cat out of his face!"

Brian backed off. He squeezed the kitten between his hands so it let out a horrible cry.

"For God's sake, don't strangle it!" I cried.

"I'm *not!*" His protest was so genuine I almost doubted what I'd seen. "There, there," he crooned to the kitten. "Poor dear. That dog of yours is really vicious! He nearly scared the life out of my cat!"

"Plato wouldn't hurt a flea! It was all your fault!" I knelt and threw my arms around Plato. I could feel his body quivering, hear the low, warning growl in his chest.

Mom ran out of the house. "What's going

on?" she demanded. "What's all the noise about?"

"Plato nearly ate the kitty!" Cookie sobbed.

Mom lifted Cookie into her arms and soothed her. She glared at me. "What happened?"

"Brian tried to sic the cat on Plato! I told him this is Plato's turf, that he should go easy, but he wouldn't listen! He wanted this to happen!"

"That's ridiculous, Aunt Barbara. I didn't do a thing. Just look at this sweet little furball. All I did was show her to Plato and he spooked. He's a killer, Aunt Barbara. Take my word for it. You better not let him out of the yard; he's dangerous!"

"Liar! Liar!" I yelled.

"Stop that!" Mom warned.

"I'm not lying. Honest!" Brian went on. "Ask Cookie, Aunt Barbara. She was here!"

Cookie buried her head deeper in Mom's shoulder and broke into a new round of sobbing. Mom smoothed her hair and patted her back. "I thought you said cats and dogs get along together, Brian," she said.

"I did, Aunt Barbara, and they do! I don't know what got into Plato."

"I'll tell you what! It was—"

"Enough!" Mom cut me short and glared at us. "Listen you two, and listen good! I don't want this happening again. I don't want Cookie scared like this, either! If having a cat means trouble like this, then the cat has to go!"

I suppressed a happy grin.

Brian's eyes narrowed. He gazed thoughtfully off into the distance, while he stroked the kitten rhythmically, hypnotically. "It won't happen again, Aunt Barbara. I promise," he said, earnestly. "But I have to ask you something."

"Yes?"

"I have to know." Brian took a long, deep breath, then asked, "Does that mean—if Tim and I don't get along, I'll have to go, too?"

Mom's face turned as deep red as the bougainvillea on the wall behind her. "Oh, Brian, dear. No. Of course not. How could you ever think that? Of course you'd never have to leave."

"Thanks," he whispered. "I needed to hear that." Brian bit his lip, and studied the ground as if he felt genuinely grateful.

Mom didn't see it, but I did. He was hiding a smile.

12

"My goodness! It was never like this in my day! What's wrong with society?" Mom exclaimed when we came down for breakfast a few mornings later. She programmed the microwave to heat her coffee and stood by, reading the paper as the time ticked away.

"What's happening to society, Aunt Barbara?" Brian asked, playing to Mom's attention.

Society's ills was one of my mother's favorite subjects. She volunteered at a mental health clinic and took each of the sad stories she heard to heart—the abused child, the druggie teenager, the homeless schizophrenic, all the fault of society's lack of concern. I shook breakfast cereal into my bowl and shut my eyes, not ready to face the world and all its problems.

Mom came back to the table, head bent over the paper. "This is awful, just awful."

"What's awful?" I asked.

"Crime. Vandalism. Senseless violence! The sheriff's column is full of it. Someone spray painted a house under construction in that new subdivision. Graffiti all over the wall! The second time this month! Now who'd do a thing like that?" Mom shook her head in dismay.

"Do they have any idea who did it?" Brian asked.

"Police say they left their signature—a thunderbolt. Probably kids from out of the community."

Sure. I lowered my eyes, afraid she'd see my face. Had Brian gone back another time, alone?

"And listen to this," Mom went on. "Someone's poisoning cats in the neighborhood! Poisoning *cats,* for heaven's sake. Sick, that's what it is. Sick!"

"This your work, Brian?" I asked, only half joking.

"Funny guy." He gave me a lopsided smirk and continued to smear peanut butter on a bagel. "I better keep Puff indoors from now on. Wouldn't want anyone poisoning *her*!" he said.

"Better keep Plato locked in the yard, too," I added, looking directly at Brian.

"And listen to *this*," Mom interrupted. "Two robberies last week, just blocks from here."

"That's terrible! That's really terrible." Brian exclaimed. "You need a security system, Aunt Barbara. Where I used to live everyone had one! I know about those things."

"Plato's our security system," I muttered.

"Yeah, sure. He's afraid of a cat. But, you know what? I could train him to be a guard dog! He'd be good at it! What do you think?"

"Just leave my dog alone, understand? Keep your cotton pickin' fingers off him!" I shouted.

Brian held up both hands. "Cool it, cuz. I was just trying to help!"

"Enough, you two!" Mom warned. "You're always bickering. Now finish breakfast and get going or you'll be late for school!"

All through the school day, no matter what I did, I felt like a worm was feasting on my insides. I wished Brian had never come to live with us. He'd eaten his way into my whole life. Cookie adored him. Gina saw him as a sad romantic hero. Mom and Dad pitied and protected him. They hated my snide remarks and coldness toward him. Had I no compassion? Wasn't I being a bit selfish? Could there be just a little jealousy, perhaps?

Maybe they'd have understood if I could have brought myself to tell them about the joy ride, the shoplifting, the vandalism. But I couldn't. They'd be so hurt.

I stared out the window in math class, a million miles away, suspecting Brian of terrible things. Not just lying and stealing, but worse, much worse. Breaking into people's homes, maybe. Killing cats. Setting fire to his own home and parents, maybe!

My God! Did I hate him so much I could suspect even that? It was the stuff of Stephen King novels.

Then, when I'd be thinking the worst, I'd wonder—how could everyone else be wrong and only me right?

Outside, dark clouds threatened rain, a rain that seemed sure but probably wouldn't come, as often happened. Maybe my suspicions were like that, dark and threatening, but without substance. How could I prove what I didn't want to believe—that Brian was more than just a prankster. That he had no conscience. That he was—I couldn't believe I was thinking this—*evil*.

"Gordon's talking to you!" Brian nudged me.

I swung around to face the blackboard covered with symbols and equations that made no sense. Mr. Gordon, in front of the board, held a textbook in one hand and a chalk in the other. "What do you say, Tim? Can you help us out here? What should we do next?"

Brian scribbled something on a sheet of paper and turned the page for me to see. The symbols meant nothing. My face began to burn as I felt everyone's eyes on me.

"Well, Tim? Are you with us?"

"Sorry, Mr. Gordon. My mind kind of wandered."

"Too bad. You won't learn a thing on cloud

nine." He made a mark in his grade book and called on someone else.

For the rest of the period I tried to focus, took faithful notes, kept my eyes on Gordon. But it was hopeless. When the bell rang I closed my notebook on equations that made no sense. Still, I felt better than when I came into class because in the margin of my book I'd scribbled three questions: *Grandma? Where does he go? What does he do?* I planned a course of action to find out the truth.

I would write Grandma and follow Brian. Maybe then I'd know if my suspicions were correct.

Brian fell in beside me as we left the classroom. "Gotta pay attention in Gordon's class. You told me that the first day, remember, cuz?"

"Don't rub it in."

"Sorry. Listen. You can copy my notes tonight and I'd be glad to explain if you have any questions. He's testing us on the stuff tomorrow."

His unexpected thoughtfulness caught me by surprise. I felt a twinge of guilt at accepting help while planning to expose him. "Thanks."

"*De nada.*" He smiled that peculiar nonsmile that always seemed false, looked away, and we continued down the hall. "Hey, look who's here today! Gordon's kid. Hi, Mitch!"

"You know his name?"

"I know *lots* of things."

Gordon's son stopped in front of us, pale,

moon faced, with lashless, slanted eyes. He wore a big smile, but showed no sign of recognition.

"Gonna see your daddy, Mitch?" Brian asked above the noise in the hall.

"Yeah."

Kids around us pushed by, looking at us funny. I stepped aside. What was Brian up to now, befriending a kid like Mitch? Did he think it would get him in better with Gordon?

"Here, Mitch. This is for you." Brian drew a Mars bar from his pocket and held it out.

"My mama said, 'Don't take candy from strangers.' "

"I'm not a stranger, Mitch. I'm a friend of your daddy's."

"Oh, then that's okay." Mitch took the candy and unwrapped it slowly. "I like Mars bars," he said. "They're good."

Brian patted his arm. "Enjoy, Mitch. See you later." He strolled on down the hall, whistling.

"What was *that* about?"

"Can't a guy be nice to a poor retard without a motive?" He left me openmouthed and confused, staring after him. *"Sayonara,"* he called over his shoulder.

I sat in my room that night, doing other homework while waiting for Brian to come up to explain the math I missed.

Just when I thought I'd figured him out, he surprised me—like offering to help with math. Like being kind to Mitch and playing with

Cookie. I heard their voices now, downstairs—Brian's deep one and Cookie's light laughter. They were teasing Puff with a ball of twine.

Maybe some of what I felt *was* envy. Brian got better grades while hardly trying. It made me feel stupid because I had to work hard to get an A or B. "Maybe he's ahead because schools back East are harder than in California," Gina had said, trying to make me feel better.

"Maybe he's just a lot smarter," I said.

I tuned out the laughter and opened my notebook to a blank sheet. With Brian downstairs it seemed a good time to start that letter to Grandma.

"Dear Grams," I wrote, then chewed on the cap of my ballpoint pen for a long time. What should I say? How do you ask important, prying questions without seeming to?

"I haven't written since we got back from New Haven because of school and stuff," I wrote. "But you asked me to keep in touch and tell you how it's going with Brian, so here I am.

"Brian's in some of my classes. He's a good student, better than me. (Or is it—I?) He's pretty much a loner. Mom says it takes time to make friends in a new place and probably she's right. He says he writes you, so you probably know all that."

I chewed the pen some more because now I'd reached the hard part. Now I needed to ask the questions Grandma might think strange.

"We have a project in English to write about someone we know," I wrote. I squirmed a little at the lie but couldn't figure any other way to learn what I wanted without giving away my suspicions. "We have to write about 'the forces that influenced' that person. I chose to write about Brian because I don't know him very well even though we room together.

"You saw him growing up, even cared for him the first couple of years because Aunt Linda worked. Tell me about him. Did he have friends? A girlfriend? What was he like as a child? You can tell a lot about a kid from the trouble he gets into. What kind of trouble did Brian make?"

I stopped and reread what I'd written and almost crossed out the last sentence. Grandma might see right through it. Could she admit to me that Brian had problems? After all, he was *her* grandchild, too.

"Brian's kind of a puzzle to me and because we're cousins, I want to understand him. I've asked him about his past but he's vague, or else clams up. You're the only one I know who knew him well, so that's why I'm turning to you.

"Could you answer soon? And Grandma? Please don't mention my letter to Brian when you write him. He'd be furious."

I reread the whole letter and decided it was the best I could do. I had just begun addressing the envelope when Brian came into the room. He tossed Puff on his bed and came to the desk.

Hurriedly, I slid the envelope into my math book and looked up.

"So, what are you up to?" Brian asked, eyes flitting quickly to the book I now clutched against my chest. "Get a chance to go over those math notes yet?"

"Yeah, uh—n-no," I stammered, feeling my face begin to burn. "I was waiting for you."

"Well, here I am, cuz." A small smile lit his face, and I had the oddest feeling he knew what I'd been doing. He pulled up a chair and reached for the math book. What if the letter fell out?

"Okay, cuz, let's get started," Brian said.

13

"Turner must be sick," Brian remarked as we went through the parking lot at school the next day.

"Why?"

"Her car's gone. See? Her parking space is empty."

"Oh, yeah!" Awareness of who parked where in the school lot was not high on my interest list. Still, Turner's red convertible with its canvas cover was something you noticed. "Maybe she took the car in for repair or something," I said.

"Yeah, maybe." Brian peeled off to wherever he usually went for the ten minutes or so before first period and I jogged off to find Gina. She waved at me from the balcony overlooking the campus and I took the steps two at a time to reach her.

"Did you hear the news?"

I smiled at her excitement and put an arm

around her shoulder. "You got the part you wanted in *Fiddler on the Roof!*"

She nudged me with a hip. "No, silly! I won't know about that till Friday. I mean the news about Turner!"

Something cold ran down my spine, and I stopped to look at her. "What news?" I'd seen the school counselor just yesterday. She'd stopped me in the hall to ask how things were going with Brian. "Is she sick or something?"

"No, she's okay, but her Porsche isn't. When she came to get it last night she found someone had ripped off the canvas cover and spray painted all over the leather seats and all over the outside. And they left a *dead cat* on the floor! She's devastated!"

Brian, I thought instantly. And who'd believe it?

"Aren't you going to *say* anything?" Gina asked. A whiff of cafeteria lunch came on the breeze and nearly turned my stomach.

"Poor Turner." I shook my head, knowing how much the counselor loved that car. And— poor cat. "Do they know who did it?"

"Some kids are blaming a Latino gang because they sign their graffiti with a lightning bolt. That's what they found on the hood."

"*A lightning bolt?*" I swung around to face Gina, heart thumping wildly. The lightning bolt was Brian's signature! It *had* to be him. "There's something I have to tell you." I gripped her arms, ready now to talk about the afternoon at the building site. She might lose all respect for me but at least she'd understand.

"Shh. Here comes Brian." Gina's eyes brightened.

Brian rounded the corner and headed straight for us, tall, good-looking, well built. You could sense a stir among the girls nearby.

"You guys hear about Turner's Porsche?"

"Everyone's talking about it," Gina said. "What did you hear?"

"I know who did it."

"Who?" we both exclaimed in astonishment. Kids nearby stopped talking and turned to listen.

"Mitch, Gordon's kid!"

"I *don't* believe it," I cried.

"I don't, either," Gina agreed. "He's the sweetest, most good-natured—"

"You *better* believe it! They've got proof!" Brian's eyes went dark, unreadable. I felt a kind of nervous energy about him, like he was coming off a high.

"Yeah? What kind? They'd have to catch him in the act for me to believe it!" I said, scornfully.

"Exactly! They did. Caught him in the act!"

Gina and I stared in shock at each other.

"It's true! Turner found him right there, sitting in the driver's seat with an empty can of spray paint in hand, going 'zzzzz, zzzz' like the noise the paint makes when it comes out of the can."

"Jeez!" I said. "He'd kill a cat?"

Brian nodded. "Turner cried, really bawled. She just put her head down on the hood and cried her heart out!"

"Jeez."

"And you know what else?" Brian chuckled. "Guess who was with her when she came out and saw all that?"

"Who?" Gina asked.

"Oh, God, poor Mitch!" I cried. "Gordon."

Brian nodded, really enjoying the impact he'd had on us. "That's *right*! His own father, Mr. Gordon. Now, isn't that a blast?"

So Brian hadn't done it.

Or had he?

The more I thought of it, the less I could see Mitch Gordon planning a wicked act like that. Couldn't see him deliberately killing a cat and then dropping him in a car. All that took planning. He'd have to go out and buy the paint, wait till the campus was deserted, have the sense to remove the canvas car cover. If he could think that far, then he wouldn't be dumb enough to sit around and wait to be caught.

No. It was a setup. It was Brian. He knew Mitch didn't have the smarts to finger the real culprit. I'd bet my life on it. I feared Brian now more than I hated him.

"I have something to tell you," I told Gina

after lunch. "Private. Come on." I took her hand and walked her to the playing field and then up the stairs to the top level of the bleachers.

"Okay, now what's so private, Mr. Mysterious, that you have to drag me way up here to tell me?" Gina dropped down on the hard seat beside me, out of breath.

"It's about Brian. I think *he,* not Mitch, vandalized Turner's car."

"There you go again! Tim Anderson! Will you please stop picking on your poor cousin? For heaven's sake, they *caught* Mitch!"

"Will you please just listen?"

She clasped her hands with disbelieving patience and glared at me.

"Maybe you'll never want to have anything to do with me again when you hear what I did—but . . ." I told her about that day at the building site, how Brian had signed his graffiti with a thunderbolt. "A thunderbolt. Get it? Just like on the hood of Turner's car!"

I told her how weird it had seemed when he made up to Mitch. "To gain his confidence! Don't you see? Now do you believe me? Do you?"

Gina frowned. "I don't know. Maybe. It's all circumstantial. I mean—it was terrible what you guys did, but it doesn't prove it."

"What about the thunderbolts?"

"I don't know. I've seen kids in study hall with thunderbolts on their notebooks. . . ." She stared at me, silent, maybe a little doubtful. "There's no motive. I mean—why? Why would he do such a mean thing?"

"Maybe he's got a screw loose."

"No way! Brian's as normal as you or me. Look. He called me a few times and we've talked. He's kind of nice, really."

"He called you? And you didn't tell me?"

"I didn't want to make trouble. I knew you'd just get angry. I know how you feel about him. Is it such a crime? He needed someone to talk to, that's all!"

"What a rat! Of all people, he had to pick on *my* girlfriend, huh? Boy, I'm pissed. What did you two talk about?"

Gina looked pained. "I shouldn't say. I wouldn't tell him what we talk about, but well . . . he had a rough time in New Haven. His parents should never have had him, he said. They cared more about their work, had no patience, always made him feel like a burden. They'd accuse him of things he never did. Sent him to summer camps to be rid of him. Things like that."

"The only thing I believe in all that is that they didn't trust him—with good reason!"

"There you go again!"

The bell rang signaling end of lunch. We both turned to the sound. I stood up. "Let's go."

"Tim, please! Don't be angry!"

"My cousin's a liar, a thief, and maybe even

a murderer, and you don't believe me. I shouldn't be angry?"

Gina raced down the bleacher steps after me. "He can't be what you say! I can't believe that! Brian's a very private person. That's what makes him seem different. Maybe he does do a few devilish things, for attention, maybe. But he's not a criminal. Tim, listen! Stop running away!"

I glanced back. "He's *evil!*"

"Oh, Tim." Her voice was full of so much disappointment that it hurt.

"He's evil, and I'm going to prove it!"

14

I left the house before Brian that night, mumbling that I had stuff to do at the library. I left him sitting cross-legged on his bed, stroking Puff, Walkman plugged into his ears. He'd changed to the black, long-sleeved shirt he wore whenever he went out at night. This time, when he left, I'd be ready.

My heart beat faster as I stood across the street from my own home, hidden in the shadow of a big California oak, watching. The lights were on in Dad's study, so he'd be reading or working. I heard the faint discordant sounds of the piano, so Mom would be in the living room while Cookie practiced. A dog barked without stop a few blocks away. I had come to this—spying on Brian. It wasn't right, but how else could I prove what no one would believe?

With eyes fastened on the front door I almost missed him. Brian slipped out of the side gate leading to the pool area, crossed the lawn, avoiding the lights along the walk, and gained the street. Mom and Dad would not even know he was gone. Without a backward glance, he strode briskly away. I let him get a half block ahead, then left my hiding place and followed.

Was Brian just out for a stroll? Maybe back East people took walks after dark, but not where we lived in California. What was he up to? Where did he go nights while I sat studying? Was he responsible for the robberies? For the poisoned cats? Maybe tonight I'd find out.

The fog began to roll in as it usually did this time of night. Smelling of brine, it smudged the houses, swirled around the streetlamps and bushes, and played hide-and-seek with Brian. Not wanting to lose him, I swept the dampness from my eyes and quickened my pace. A dog barked a warning as I approached and passed his territory. "Shhh!" I whispered, fearful Brian would notice and look back.

From time to time Brian stopped before a house, stood watching it for a time, then moved on. Once, he peered over the fence into a backyard for a long time. Was he feeding poison to some animal in the yard? I crept closer, my heart in my mouth, but just as I was about to cross the street, he turned and I ducked behind a tree.

I'd followed him for almost a mile when he paused before a dark house, slipped into a shadow, and disappeared. I waited, holding my breath, eyes glued to the last place I'd seen him. Dare I move closer? My palms were sweaty and cold. What if he caught me following him?

A car drove by, first lighting the road with a thick, yellow glow, then blocking my view.

"Jeez!" I cursed into the still darkness when it had passed. I darted across the road and hid behind a tree, straining to see through the fog. Tree by tree I advanced, peering into the mist. Where was he? Had he moved on, or could he have broken into that dark house?

Forcing myself forward, I ran across the lawn, ducked down near some bushes, and listened. Did I really hear the tinkle of glass breaking, or was that the pulse pounding in my ears? I parted a bush and stood on tiptoe to peek inside. Was that a light moving in the hall beyond the room?

My heart flipped at a sound behind me and I nearly fell as I swung around.

"What are *you* doing here?"

Brian! "Jeez! You scared the daylights out of me! Turn that thing off! I can't see!" I whispered, blocking my eyes from the blinding beam of his flashlight.

Brian kept the beam on my face. "What are *you* doing here? This isn't the way to the library." There was a cold threat in his tone.

"I, er . . . I, er, decided to take a walk instead. Damn it, Brian! Turn that light off!" I whispered.

He clicked off the flashlight. "You're lying.

You've been following me. Checking on me! What did you think I was doing?"

"W-well, er," I stammered, unable to see clearly now and trying to find a plausible answer to his question. "Hey, let's get out of here before someone sees us and calls the police."

He switched the flashlight on again, aiming it at my face. "I ought to snuff you, following me like this, you know that? What do you think I was up to, huh?"

"All *right*! Yeah, I followed you! I wanted to know what you do when you go out nights! Now, put out that light and let's get out of here!"

He gripped my arm. "Just what do you *think* I do?"

A car approached and passed, its beam gliding over us for a moment. He was bigger and stronger than me. He could overpower me, kill me maybe. I couldn't let my mind dwell on the possibility. Scared as I was, I shook off his grasp. "I figure you're doing something rotten. Robbing houses. Killing cats! That's what I think!"

Brian advanced a step, forcing me against the prickly bushes. "You're not even a good spy! I knew you were following me from the first dog's bark!"

Cornered and shaking, but infuriated by his contempt, I blurted, "You *are* the one, aren't you? You're the one we're reading about in the papers!"

"Man, you're so sick with envy, it's not even

funny," Brian said. "I'm invading your territory and you don't like it one bit."

"What were *you* doing nosing around this house, huh?" I asked, growing angrier by the second.

He snorted. "Poor guy. Can't even add two and two so how could you expect to know. I caught *you* in the act, didn't I?" He paused to let that sink in. Then he added, "Did it ever occur to you that maybe you have it all wrong? That instead of a villain I could be a hero?"

"Oh, sure!"

"You want to know why I'm cruising around nights? Well, I'll tell you. While *you're* reading books, I'm out here risking my neck. I *know* this neighborhood. Even the dogs don't bark anymore when I pass. I'm gonna catch those burglars and that cat killer, too. If you hadn't been on my tail, maybe I'd have found them tonight! And that— cuz—is why I'm out nights!"

Could it be? I opened my mouth, then shut it. Of all the possible reasons Brian might have given, not once had I considered this. The skin on the back of my neck prickled. Could it be? If so, I owed him a huge apology but couldn't bring myself to say it.

"I'm going home now. Coming?" Brian strode back across the lawn to the sidewalk. In a moment I caught up and fell in step beside him. "Listen," he said. "I'm not the monster you think. I'm not, honest, so stop checking on me, okay? We're blood relatives after all. Trust me."

I wanted to. I really did.

But I didn't.

If I couldn't follow Brian without giving myself away, and with no word from Grandma yet—I was stuck. There seemed no way to prove Brian was not what he seemed to be. Unless, I thought, pacing my room one night after Brian had left—*unless* there was evidence!

"Yes!" I clamped a hand over my mouth and looked toward the hall. If Brian was responsible for the robberies, he might have *kept* something that would give him away.

I closed my bedroom door and leaned against it, breathing fast. Puff lay sleeping on the floor near the window. Brian's half of the room was as neat and uncluttered as a monk's cell. He had his own desk, chair, and dresser. On the desk were two books, a yellow legal pad, a black cup with pencils and pens, and a stapler. Except for a comb and brush, his dresser was naked.

What I was about to do was wrong and sneaky, something I'd never have done before Brian came into my life. But I didn't care.

I went to the desk first. The center drawer contained pencils, stamps, new boxes of staples—lost in the big space. The next drawer was empty and the one below held typing paper, envelopes, and paper clips. Nothing of interest. I was about to open the next drawer when I noticed the edge of a file folder sticking out below the paper. I drew it out and opened it. Inside I found a number of clippings from our local newspaper. An article about a fire that nearly destroyed the General Store. An opinion piece by a psychologist on the kind of person who might poison cats. Weekly sheriff reports on vandalism and thefts.

Weird. Not the kind of stuff anyone I knew would keep, but not proof. He could explain it away by saying he was the lone vigilante seeking the people who committed these crimes. I slid the folder back under the typing paper, and opened the last drawer. Also empty. I closed it and, disappointed, stared at the desk.

What about the books on top? I riffled the pages of Brian's history text and French book. Nothing inside. I flipped through the blank pages of the yellow pad. Nothing.

The wastepaper basket! I emptied its contents on the desk and sorted through the crumpled papers. Some math problems worked out and tossed. An English essay on *Romeo and Juliet* across which the teacher had written: Well done. A sheet with Gina's name written in different style prints and thunderbolts drawn in different sizes. Five empty matchbooks.

I held one to my nose and closed my eyes. It brought back that night in New Haven. I could imagine Brian setting fire to the boxes behind the General Store. I could imagine him setting fire to his own house. My God. How paranoid! Who sounded more off his rocker now?

"Tim?" Mom knocked at the door. She turned the knob. I hurriedly swept the debris back into the basket and set the basket back on the floor. Guiltily I called, "Yeah, Mom?"

"Why'd you lock the door? Open up! I've got some news for you and Brian!"

Mom stood at the door, smiling. "Just heard from Grandma! She's leaving on an elder-hostel tour of Japan and she's coming here first. Isn't that wonderful?"

"*Great*! When?"

"Day after tomorrow!" Mom peeked around me. "Where's Brian?"

"Out."

"Well be sure to tell him when he gets back. I'm sure he'll be delighted."

"Yeah."

I closed the door and listened to Mom's footsteps going down the hall. Grandma would be here soon! I'd never gotten an answer to my letter. Now I could ask in person.

Puff awoke, stretched, and ambled over to me. She rubbed her body against my legs and mewed contentedly. I bent, stroked her back absentmindedly, then left her. Time to go back to work.

I opened Brian's top dresser drawer. Such neatness! *My* clothes were stuffed in drawers too full to close. Pajamas and shorts, sweaters and unmatched socks, all jumbled together. I could never find what I wanted right away. Brian's underwear and socks lay folded and stacked as precisely as if he'd been trained in the army.

I lifted each item and set it exactly back in place. I even squeezed folded socks, expecting to feel something hard, something that shouldn't be there, but found nothing.

Maybe there *was* nothing to find.

I pulled open the next drawer. All sweaters. Nothing else. And the bottom drawer—sweats, perfectly folded.

"Puff!" I exclaimed in dismay as the cat leaped from the bed to Brian's desk, making a clatter as she knocked over his pencil cup. "Get off there!" I grabbed the cat and tossed it to the floor, then picked up the spilled pens and pencils and righted the cup. No use in giving Brian reason for suspicion, even if it was the cat's fault.

I'd already begun to dig through the contents of the last drawer—when I straightened, puzzled, looking back to the desk. Something in the cup, something bright, had caught my eye.

I flew back to Brian's desk and dumped the contents of the black cup on the yellow pad. Pencils, pens, two paper clips, a marble, and—what was this? The Christmas tree brooch Dad had given Mom last Christmas! The brooch Mom said must have cost Dad a month's salary. My mouth went dry. I felt so good I could have danced. *Evi-*

dence! At last! Proof that Brian stole. Let him try to explain this away.

I checked my watch. If he followed his usual pattern, he'd be gone another half hour yet. Lots of time. Time to check the bed, the closet, maybe even under Puff's mattress. Who knew what I'd find?

15

I dropped the Christmas tree brooch back in the cup on Brian's desk. Better to leave it there and let Mom and Dad see for themselves where Brian hid it. When I heard footsteps coming up the stairs, I was kneeling on the closet floor holding one of Brian's boots. I had put my hand inside and drawn out a handful of small jewelry packets in their original wrappings. Frantic, I threw them back in the boot, shoved the boot back in place, and shut the closet door.

Breathing hard, I ran to my bed, grabbed a book, and sat down just as Brian opened the door.

"Big meeting downstairs," he remarked, coming into the room.

I could hear the voices. Mom must have been entertaining her mental health board. "Er . . . uh . . . yeah. How'd it go? Catch any thieves tonight?" My voice sounded so false that Brian had to notice.

"None," he said, eyes narrowing. "They must know I'm watching." He glanced around the room, removed his jacket, and casually hung it in the closet. Then he bent to tie his shoelace. Or was he checking the boot? My heart nearly stopped. Had I replaced the boot exactly where Brian left it?

"Nice out. Mild and clear. Full moon." Brian turned back to me. "You been in all night?"

"Ummm." I bent over my book to hide the flush I could feel rising to my face.

"Why don't you get out? Take Plato for a walk?"

"Yeah, great idea!" I jumped up, glad for a legitimate reason to leave Brian.

"Mind putting Puff out when you go, Tim?" Brian called from the bathroom. "Poor kitten's been cooped up ever since that cat poisoner struck. Should be safe now. It's been two weeks."

"Sure." I grabbed Puff and my jacket and was almost out the door when I turned and said, "By the way. Grandma's coming Friday. She'll be here overnight!" When Brian didn't answer I called, "Brian? Did you hear?"

"I heard," he finally said. "Wonderful."

A surge of adrenaline charged through me. Brian's hesitation said loads. He feared Grandma's coming. Between what I knew and what she could tell us, we'd nail him!

I left Puff in the backyard, hitched the leash to Plato, and strode happily down the street toward

Gina's house. She was the one I wanted to share the news with first. Meanwhile, I had to think through just how and how much to tell Mom and Dad when I got back.

"I know it's late, Gina, but it's very important," I said at her door. "I've got to talk to you!"

Gina checked her watch. "It's almost ten o'clock, Tim. Dad?" she called back to her father. "Tim's here. We want to go outside a few minutes. We'll just be in front. Okay?"

"Ten minutes!" her father called. "And then I want you in the house!"

We sat on the top step of the stoop. I let Plato off the leash to sniff around the bushes. The moonlight was so bright that when Gina turned to me I could see her face.

"I need to try this out on you before I talk to my parents," I said, starting right away. "I found some things in my room that prove Brian steals."

"Oh, *no!*" Gina covered her cheeks with her hands.

She frowned off into space as I went on to tell her everything. When I finished I said, "Now you play devil's advocate. Can I possibly be wrong?"

"There's *got* to be an explanation," she said, after berating me for snooping into Brian's things.

"An explanation? Oh boy, Gina! What's with you? You're always finding excuses for him!"

"Stop that. You asked me to be devil's advocate. I'm trying to be logical. Suppose the brooch was put there by someone else?"

"Who? That sounds just like the kind of excuse *he'd* give! Who'd go into Mom's things, take her best piece of jewelry, and drop it in Brian's pencil holder? That's ridiculous!"

"Well, maybe." Gina tilted her head and regarded me with a look of suspicion. "You're too quick to condemn him. There *could* be some logical answer."

"No! And no logical reason for all those things in his boot, either."

"Maybe he *bought* them. Have you thought of that? From—a street vendor, maybe. They sell stuff very cheap. A dollar or two for earrings and tie clips and things like that, real cheap."

"Oh, sure. In their original wrappings? That's not street-vendor junk. No way! Besides, why would he want stuff like that? And then hide it in a boot when he has all that empty drawer space? Explain that!"

We sat silent for a long, angry moment, then I repeated the question that still didn't have an answer. "What could he possibly want with all those pins and earrings and brooches and bracelets? He's a guy. He doesn't wear things like that!"

"Gifts?"

"Come *on* . . ."

"There has to be *some* reason. I can't believe he's a thief."

"I *can*."

"Oh, Tim." She sounded so disappointed in me. "Are you really going to tell your parents?"

"I was. Now I don't know. I've got to think about it some more. He's spooky. I never know what he might do next, and if he kills cats, maybe he could kill—"

"Stop that! What's gotten into you? This is real life, not a horror novel! There's no proof Brian killed anything, and poisoning cats is a long way from hurting people. I can't believe this— you're obsessed with Brian!"

I hadn't expected such a lecture and didn't answer.

"My ten minutes are up. I've got to go in." Gina stood, crossing her arms over her chest, like she didn't want me to touch her. "Don't tell your parents, Tim. Don't do that to Brian. He's already lost so much. If he's innocent and he thinks he's lost your family's trust, too, it would be so awful."

"He's guilty! I know he is! And of much more than just stealing!"

"I give up!" Gina swung by me and was up the stairs and inside her house before I could answer. "Let me know how it turns out." She closed the door behind her without looking back.

Furious, I collected Plato and jogged home. I'd expected Gina to side with me, to see the facts as I did, to say: You're right. Brian *is* a nut case.

You better tell your parents because there's nothing *you* can do.

She hadn't. I knew her well enough to know she didn't think I made up the theft story but truly believed Brian could explain. She also probably figured I was desperate to discredit Brian because I was no longer top dog in the family. How's that for a crock?

By the time I reached our block I was so mad I left Plato in the yard, sprinted up the back stairs to our room, and slammed the door behind me. "Okay, Brian," I said, out of breath. "It's time we talked!"

He'd been lying in bed, hands under his head, staring up at the ceiling. Smiling, he sat up and propped his pillow behind his back. "Oh, yeah? What about?"

I took a deep breath. "You. About what you've been doing. I can't stop what you do outside our house but I can sure stop you doing anything harmful here. This is my home, my family, and I'm not going to let you hurt us."

"What are you talking about, Tim?" Brian stretched and yawned.

"You know, all right. I'm talking about your stealing! About bringing your loot home and hiding it in our house!" I went to this desk and dumped the pencil cup out on the yellow pad. Mom's brooch, sparkling with red and green stones, fell out. I held it up. "I'm talking about this! What's it doing in your pencil cup? This is Mom's! It cost Dad a lot of money. What are you doing with it?"

"I haven't the faintest idea." Brian lifted one shoulder lazily and dropped it.

"Don't give me that!" My voice grew shrill. "It's there because you put it there! You stole it!"

"Unh-unh. I sure didn't. I'm not that dumb. If I had, think I'd put it in such an obvious place?" His eyes opened wide, questioning. "You know what? Maybe Cookie did it. She comes in here a lot. She likes to play with Puff—sits at my desk sometimes to use my colored ink pens. Maybe she saw the pin on your mom's bureau one day, picked it up to play with, didn't know its value. You know kids. Maybe she brought it with her when she came in here and dumped it in my cup. How should I know? But *I* didn't take it." He scratched his head calmly and gazed off at the cat bed. "Did you see Puff in the yard when you came in?"

"Cookie comes in here—with you, *alone*?" I heard a note of hysteria in my voice. "Mom allows it?"

"Sure. Sometimes your mom goes marketing. I keep an eye on her. Anything wrong with that?" He smiled. "Have you seen Puff? I called her, but she hasn't come back since you put her out. I'm worried."

"No!" Distracted by a swarm of ugly, half-formed visions of Brian alone with my sister, I shivered and tried to get back to the subject.

Gina had warned that there could be logical reasons for what I'd found. Well, let's see what Brian made of all that jewelry he'd hidden in his boot. My anger rose again. "Maybe you can explain away the brooch," I said, heading for the closet, "but what about all that loot you've got hidden in your boot, huh?"

Brian had gotten up and gone to the doors looking out to the pool area to call Puff. "Loot? What are you talking about, Tim? Have you gone off your rocker?" He came back to where I sat on my haunches on the floor of the closet, reaching for his boots.

"Tim? What are you doing, Tim! Are you nuts?"

"See!" I yanked his boots out of the closet and turned them both upside down at once, an expectant, gleeful grin already beginning on my lips. Even as I lifted the boots I knew the grin was premature. The boots were empty. Empty! Brian must have sensed from my guilty face when he came into the room earlier what I'd been up to. Sure. He'd been the one to say "It's such a nice night. Why don't you take Plato for a walk!" So he could get rid of the evidence. And I fell for it! *Dork!* I felt so much hate I could have killed him.

"Something wrong? he asked, softly.

"Where'd you hide them, you creep?" I

jumped to my feet and punched him in the face with all I had. I got in one good punch before he grabbed my arms and held me off.

"Do that again, wussy, and you're gone," he whispered, "and that's not an idle threat." He touched the place I'd made bleed. "Listen good. There's nothing in my boot because there was nothing to find. I don't steal. I'm no crook. I'm not a liar. I didn't take your mother's brooch. If you think I did, ask Cookie.

"Now I'm gonna let you go 'cause I got much more important things to do. Puff's not back and I'm worried. That cat killer may be on the prowl again. So cool it, cuz. Go tattle to your parents if you want, but who's gonna believe you? Where's your evidence? Me? I'm going out now to find my cat!"

"I'll get you, Brian," I yelled after him as he left the room. "I swear, I'll get you! You'll mess up eventually, and then—watch out!"

Brian turned back, eyes narrowed. So softly that I almost didn't hear, he said, "Not before I get *you*!"

16

When Brian left to find Puff I dropped onto my bed, hands clenched into fists, barely stopping the urge to scream.

I should have asked him about all those matches, about the fire at the General Store.

I should have warned him to keep matches away from Cookie! Shoot! Maybe he was already letting her play with them.

I should have questioned him about the graffiti with his signature—the thunderbolt that others were being blamed for—the vandalism to the counselor's car . . .

But what was the use? He'd deny it all—or if he did admit it, he'd deny it later to Mom and Dad. He could talk the devil into believing him.

Again, it all came down to proof. Without absolute positive proof, proof Brian couldn't lie his way out of, the evil would continue.

I'd start by asking Cookie if she really took

the brooch, and when Grandma came, I'd take her aside and get some answers. One other thing—I couldn't tell Mom *not* to leave Cookie with Brian without good reason. But I could sure keep watch over Cookie even it it meant skipping soccer practice or afternoons with Gina.

I went into the bathroom to brush my teeth when Plato began barking. At first I didn't take much notice. He sometimes barked at strange animals or people going by. But then I realized it wasn't his usual bark, but something menacing and vicious.

I raced down the back stairs into the yard, flipping on the switches as I ran. The floodlights lit up the pool area, the umbrella tables and chairs, the garden. Off to the side where the barking came from, I saw Plato on his hind legs pawing the wood gate that led out to the front. His hackles bristled as he growled and snapped at something on the other side. I ran across the lawn and grabbed him by the collar.

"Down boy!" I commanded. "Down!" I peered over the fence. "Who's there?"

"Get that dumb dog of yours out of the way!" Brian yelled from the other side. "Damn him! I'm trying to get in and he won't let me!"

"What's going on here?" Dad came running.

"It's me, Uncle Bill! Hurry! Let me in! I've got Puff. Something's wrong!" Brian's voice had suddenly changed from threatening to pathetic. "Oh, please! Hurry!"

"Here, Dad, take Plato!" I dragged Plato, still snarling and barking, back to my father, opened the gate latch, and swung the gate wide. Brian rushed in cradling Puff.

"She's sick. I think she's been poisoned! Plato wouldn't let us in! He acted crazy! Oh, God! I think Puff's dying!"

I stood aside, worried for Puff, but not sure what to think.

"Bring her to the light." Dad motioned to a table near where he'd tied up Plato. "Quiet!" he shouted at my dog. "Tim, go inside and get some towels."

I ran into the bathroom and grabbed two big towels, folding them into a sort of bed as I ran back. I laid them on the patio table. Brian placed Puff on them and Dad bent over her. The kitten immediately threw up and then went into convulsions. Her eyes looked funny, and her tongue had lost its healthy pink.

Brian turned away and covered his face with his hands. "I thought for sure it would be safe to let her out," he cried. "Will she be okay? Is she breathing? When I couldn't find her in the yard I went looking for her. Is she going to die? I'll never forgive myself!"

Mom had heard the commotion and ran out. She tried to comfort Brian with words and touch, but Brian shook her off and turned away from her, from all of us.

What an actor, I thought, as I watched from

the sidelines. And what timing! Right when I might go to Mom and Dad with my accusations. Who'd believe such a caring, grieving guy could do any of the things I'd accuse him of?

"I don't think she'll make it," Dad whispered to Mom. "We better get her to the vet." He wrapped the kitten in his sweater and lifted her gently while Mom went to get the car keys. "Let's go, Brian. We're taking Puff to the vet. He'll know what to do. It'll be all right, son; now come along. Tim, you stay with Cookie."

I followed them to the garage and watched them get into the car and drive away, and then I went back to the house.

The house seemed so empty and lonely with Mom and Dad gone. I noticed sounds I'd never heard before, the clock ticking in the hall, a dripping faucet, the refrigerator cycling, the heater going on and off, a creaky sound in the wallboards.

I opened Cookie's door to check on her. She lay on her side hugging her white teddy bear, smiling. My heart hurt for her. She adored Puff. Puff was more her cat than Brian's. She fed her, played with her, loved her more than anyone else in the family did. I didn't want to think what would happen if Puff died.

I pulled the covers over her shoulder and went back to my own room. This time of night Brian would be on his bed, hands under his head, staring at the ceiling. Puff would be rooting around in her bed until she found just the spot she liked, then she'd curl up into a small ball and go to sleep. Where was she now? Lying on a table while the vet pumped the poison from her stomach? I swallowed a lump in my throat. Would she make it?

It would be my fault if she died! If Brian hadn't suspected I was on to him, Puff would probably still be alive and well. He was so clever, so *devious*, so *evil*, and always a step ahead of me. How could I stop him before he did something really terrible—maybe to someone in my own family?

17

Some hours later I awoke, instantly alert. In the dim light I saw Brian seated on his bed, watching me. He held what appeared to be a rope in his hands. No—it was Plato's leash! Sweat poured down my back. Every few seconds he'd snap the leash, just once, so it made a brisk, sharp, cracking sound. I didn't move, but my heart thumped so loud I thought surely he'd hear. What was he up to? Why was he watching me like that? Did he plan to strangle me?

Brian stood and stepped toward me, the leash between his hands. Terrified, I bolted upright and swung my legs off the bed, ready to fight if he came at me. "What are you doing, Brian?" I croaked, sounding more scared than challenging.

He snapped the leash rhythmically and sat back on his bed. "She's coming today. She hates me, you know. Always has."

Grandma, I thought with relief. He's scared at

what she'll tell us. So that was it. "How's Puff?" I asked, changing the subject deliberately. "Did she make it?"

"Dead." He stared straight ahead, snapping the leash and watching me.

"Gee, I'm sorry." As much as I disliked and distrusted Brian, I felt some sympathy. Was this how he mourned? I mean, what do I know about how people show loss; I'm no psychologist. Lights matches after his folks die by fire. Snaps a leather leash after his pet dies. Who knows, maybe Puff died by strangling, not poison. It was too weird for my brain.

"Let's get some sleep," I said. I lay in bed waiting for Brian's regular breathing. How many other nights had he sat up lighting matches or doing who knew what—while I slept? Creepy!

As soon as I was sure Brian was sleeping I left my bed, picked up the leash, and went looking for matches. I gathered them all into a plastic bag and zipped them into my daypack. When I got to school I'd ditch them. If Cookie spent time in my room she wouldn't have matches to play with.

When I passed Cookie's room on the way to breakfast in the morning I heard Mom's low voice and Cookie crying. I waited outside the door, fists clenched, wishing I could do something, wishing Brian had never come to our house. The door opened and Cookie came out wiping her red eyes with one hand, holding Mom's hand with the

other. I fell in step beside her and we went down
the stairs together.

"But where *is* she?" Cookie asked, looking up
at Mom. "Can't we bury her, like in that story
about Barney? And tell all the good things about
her?"

She was referring to *The Ten Best Things
About Barney,* a book I used to read her about
the death of a cat.

Mom had a catch in her voice. "Puff's already
in heaven, honey."

"But I didn't get a chance to tell her how
much I loved her!" Cookie turned to me and
started to cry again.

I heard Brian come out of our room. He
started down the stairs behind us. "I feel bad, too,
Cookie," he said. "Puff was my cat, you know."

Cookie stopped. Her forehead wrinkled as she
swung around and lifted her arms to Brian. He
picked her up. She immediately tightened her
arms around his neck, buried her face in his
shoulder, and sobbed her heart out while he
stared dry-eyed, without expression, at me.

I stared back at him, feeling a hardness like
I'd never felt toward anyone in my whole life, and
trying to disguise it. It seemed dangerous to let
him realize the depths of my distrust. He'd mes-
merized Cookie and everyone else in my family. I
wanted to take Cookie aside to ask her about
Mom's brooch, but of course not now. Not when
her heart ached so much for Puff.

"Tell you what, Cookie," I said. "We'll have a memorial service for Puff this afternoon, just like in the story about Barney. You can be thinking up ten good things about Puff while you're at preschool today. Brian and I will think up some, too, okay? And Grandma should be here by then. She can be in on it."

"Grandma will be here?" Cookie took her head off Brian's shoulder to look at me. She stopped sniffling. "Just like at Aunt Linda and Uncle Pete's funeral?" Her face brightened. "Then it will be a real funeral! Brian, did you hear? Puff will have the whole family to say good-bye!"

Brian stiffened and glanced away. He set my sister back on the floor. "I heard, Cookie. Yeah. It'll be great. We'll give Puff a real send-off!"

Grandma's face lit up and she came toward me with arms wide when I walked into the kitchen after school. I dropped my books, strode toward her, and hoisted her off the floor. "Put me down!" she cried, laughing. "Put me down, you—you—giant!" I gave her a loving squeeze, lowered her, and kissed her on top of her curly head. "What's happening to you, Grams?" I asked in a very serious tone. "Every time I see you you get shorter. Are you shrinking?"

"Oh, you!" She punched me lightly in the chest and giggled. "Come to the table. Look what I brought. Your favorite chocolates from New York. Brian's already eaten half the box."

Brian had beat me home, of course. He'd probably be around every minute to be sure I couldn't get Grandma alone. It would take some doing to find out what I needed to know. I wished I'd been there to see how Grandma had greeted *him*. Had it been as warm as my greeting, or as cautious and wary as I remembered from when we'd been in New Haven?

Mom had laid out a pot of tea and a plate of cookies. I pulled up a chair and sat beside my sister, who was trying to find the opening into a foil-covered chocolate.

"So, how long are you staying, Grams?" I asked, leaning over the chocolate box while my fingers wandered from one luscious possibility to another. I chose the biggest chewy nut.

"Only tonight. My flight leaves early tomorrow. But I'll be back in three weeks and you'll get plenty tired of me because I'll be staying for a while then."

Only overnight. When could I get Grandma alone?

"That will be great, Grandma," Brian exclaimed.

Grandma's smile faded. "I'm glad you're glad, Brian."

"It's time for Puff's memory service!" Cookie said, jumping off her chair. "Brian helped me make up a list. Come on, everyone! Let's go. Grandma, Brian, Tim, Mommy! Come!"

Cookie pulled us all out into the backyard, dragging Grandma by one hand and Brian by the other. Plato had to be in on this, too, she said, because he was also Puff's friend. And so in time we all stood under the California oak at the back of our yard. All except Dad, who had assured Cookie he'd remember Puff, though, at work in his office.

Brian took my sister's hand and the two of them walked forward a few steps, then turned to face us. "Cookie has some things to say about Puff," Brian said. He put a hand on my sister's head and said, "Go ahead, honey. Puff will know."

Cookie's brow furrowed and she touched her hands together in a prayerful position and looked up to the heavens. "Puff, this is me, Cookie. I know you're in heaven now. I didn't get to say good-bye, so if you can hear me, this is what I want to say.

"I want you to know I loved you because you were pretty and wonderfully soft and fun to play with and funny and smart ..." She stopped and looked to Brian for help, then remembered and hurriedly added, "and you were ... clean, and a good friend, and you never hurt anyone, and ... and ..." She looked puzzled. "How many is that?"

"Eight," I said.

"You were a *good* kitten. That's nine."

Cookie closed her eyes. Tears began to roll down her cheeks. In a very small voice she said, "And ten. You made me very happy."

I dug my nails into my hands, stifling the urge to sweep Cookie up and hug her. A wind blew her dark hair across her pale face. She pushed it away impatiently, then dug into a pocket and came out with her hand closed into a fist. "This is for Puff." She bent and placed a partly melted chocolate on the ground, looked at it for a moment, then started walking back to the house.

Mom and Brian fell in beside her. I heard Mom say, "That was a wonderful service, honey, really wonderful." Brian glanced back several times to see if we were following.

Grandma started after them but on the guise of handling Plato, I called, "Grandma, wait up, will you?"

She turned and waited while I put water in Plato's bowl, then I took her arm and we ambled back to the house, no longer within earshot of the others.

"I wanted to ask you something," I said, knowing I might only have a moment. "Did you get my letter before you left?"

"Letter? No. You wrote me?"

"Almost three weeks ago! You didn't get it?" A cold feeling, something like panic crept up my legs into my stomach.

"I'd have answered if I had. You know how

much I love hearing from you. Are you sure you mailed it?"

"Oh, I mailed it, all right. At least I put it in our mailbox for the postman. Unless ..." I stopped and stared at Grandma. Of course! Brian had come into the room when I'd been writing the letter! He'd seen the guilty look on my face, seen the way I'd slid the letter into my math book. All he had to do was check the mailbox for a day or two and remove the envelope before the postman arrived. That letter never left California!

"What did you write, Tim? Was it very important?"

"Very," I said. "I need to know things about Brian. And fast. I don't think we'll have much time alone. I know this is a terrible thing to ask— you being his grandma, too—but I have to know. Did he ever do anything, back in New Haven, that you think was—I don't know how else to put it except—*bad*?"

Grandma drew her arm out of mine, turned, and faced me. "Why do you want to know?" We had reached the back of the house. If we stayed too long, Brian might spring out of the house to join us.

"Things have happened, bad things, that I think Brian did, and he always has an explanation that gets him off the hook. I can't prove it, but I'm sure Brian steals; I found things. He lies; I think he stole the letter I sent you because he knows I'm on to him. He vandalized one house, maybe set fire to a building. I even think he—killed his own cat. And others." I stopped, felt heat rise to my face as I saw the look of grief on Grandma's face. "Maybe I'm wrong," I hurried on, almost ready to back down. "He was probably fine in New Haven. Maybe it's because of what happened, losing everything, everyone ... Was he fine? Do you know something I should?"

"I thought—living here in a normal environment, where he had no reputation to live down—things would be different."

"What do you mean?"

"Your parents never told you? Well, it happened years ago; it's best they didn't say. We all thought that leaving New Haven would be best for Brian. You see, dear, your cousin was always a different child, not easy to love. Even as a baby, he stiffened like a board when I tried to cuddle him. But some children are like that. I blame it all on that terrible accident eight years ago. That was the start."

"What accident?" I glanced again toward the house, worrying that Brian might interrupt any minute.

"A child drowned." Grandma wiped her eyes. "An older boy claimed Brian pushed the little girl under. Brian was only a child! If it were true, why hadn't the older boy stopped him? Brian said the boy was getting back at him for not letting him have his bicycle.

"There was never any proof and the police wrote it off as an accident, finally, but the stigma remained. Brian's aloof, some people say—cold— which made him easy prey. Boys at school, knowing of his history, picked on him. They blamed him for thefts, for loosening the wheels on a skateboard, for instance, so a classmate broke a leg—all kinds of terrible things. He became a scapegoat."

"You think Brian never did *any* of those things?"

Grandma hesitated. "No. He probably pulled the usual share of schoolboy pranks, sometimes to get back at the very boys who taunted him. He's my grandchild! He wouldn't do anything really bad! But now you're telling me it's still happening."

"Yes, Grandma, but I have no proof."

18

Brian was showering when I knocked lightly on Cookie's bedroom door early the next morning to carry down Grandma's bags. Grandma, in jeans, a zippered jacket, and sneakers, opened the door as if she'd been waiting. She held a finger to her lips, motioned me in, and closed the door behind her. Her eyes were puffy. She looked old suddenly, not like the perky lady I remembered from yesterday.

"I hardly slept for thinking of what we talked about," she whispered so as not to wake Cookie. "I hate leaving you like this—up in the air. I wanted to talk with Bill and Barbara last night but Brian was always around."

Disappointed, I whispered, "It's all right, Grandma. I have no proof, anyway."

"It isn't all right." She glanced at her watch and frowned. "The cab's due in five minutes, no time to talk with your father now. But I tell you what. I'll phone as soon as I land in Hawaii. Meanwhile, you've got to tell your parents exactly what you told me. Maybe we can get Brian some help, or get to the bottom of this."

"Okay, Grandma."

I didn't say anything about my suspicion that Brian may have set fire to his own house and may have killed his own parents. Grandma was blinded by loyalty and love. She wouldn't be able to accept that her own grandson might be a bad seed—evil to the core.

I gave her a hug. "Thanks, at least, for not thinking I'm a nut case."

She hugged me back. "Of course you're not. And neither is Brian. There's got to be a logical explanation for all this and if your parents can't get to the bottom of it, maybe I can—when I get back."

That could be too late, I thought, lifting her bags. Maybe Mom and Dad would be more objective. With what they already knew and what I could tell them, they had to realize that Brian was the opposite of what he appeared to be. But I still needed *proof.*

Proof! So much had happened so fast I hadn't had time to ask Cookie about Mom's brooch. If Cookie *hadn't* brought the brooch into our room I'd have my first real *proof.*

Right after breakfast Dad announced plans to fix the broken screen door. Mom said she had phone calls to make. Brian read the paper, but only with half attention. Now, I felt, it was up to me to decide how much had changed, if I'd gotten through to Grandma. Was Brian's cover about to be blown.

"Want to watch *Sesame Street,* Cookie?" I asked.

"Yeah!" She jumped up and ran to the TV set.

Brian yawned. "I think I'll take a ride up the coast with a friend."

What friend? I almost challenged, because he had none as far as I knew.

"Want me to make some sandwiches to take along?" Mom asked.

"My *friend*'s fixing some."

The way he emphasized "friend" set off alarms in my head. Did he mean *Gina*? He lowered his eyes and a corner of his mouth raised in a smile. It made me want to fly to the phone and ask Gina what plans she had for the day.

"What are *you* up to today, Tim?" Mom asked.

"I don't know." I gazed at my fingers, hating Brian with all my heart.

As soon as he left I found Cookie seated on the rug in front of the TV hugging Pooh-bear and watching cartoons. I plopped down beside her, pretending to watch, too. After a while I said, "Hey, Cookie, you know that pretty Christmas tree pin Dad bought Mom?"

Without taking her eyes from the screen she shook her head.

"Did you borrow it?"

She shook her head no.

I tried phrasing the question another way. "I mean, did you find it in her jewelry box and try it on and maybe play with it and take it into my room? And maybe you got busy drawing pictures on Brian's desk and left it there?"

She buried her face in Pooh-bear's fur and shook her head no again, then peered over the bear to see the TV picture.

"Cookie." I took my sister by the shoulders and turned her face toward me. "Cookie, listen. This is important. Did you take Mom's pin into my room to play? Did you put it into that pencil cup on Brian's desk?"

"No, I didn't! I told you. I didn't touch Mommy's pin. She told me never to touch her things. And I didn't!"

She was telling the truth. Later, if I asked her in front of Brian, he'd probably get her so rattled she'd say anything he wanted her to say. But now, she was telling the truth.

I patted my sister's head and stood up. The brooch was probably back in Mom's jewelry box, anyway. Brian wouldn't be so dumb as to leave it in the pencil cup after I'd shown him I knew it was there. But Mom and Dad know I don't lie. It was time to talk with them.

•   •   •

"My, isn't this mysterious," Mom said, as she took a seat in Dad's study. I'd enticed her away from her phone calls by holding a note in front of her as she talked. "Emergency. Need you." Dad came along a minute later, wiping paint from his hands with a cloth smelling of turpentine.

"What's this about, Tim?" he asked. "Not another plea for a car, I hope!"

"About Brian." All in one breath I said, "I've got things to tell you that maybe I should have said a long time ago and I hope you'll believe me and I don't know what to make of them and what to do about them and I hope you do."

And then I told them everything, from the very beginning. How first I'd joined Brian in some pranks because I'd never done anything wrong, not even in junior high when lots of kids tested the rules.

"We took your car out for a joy ride one day, Mom. I think Dad knew. Didn't you, Dad?"

I didn't wait for his answer but rushed on with the story of the General Store theft and the incident at the building site. And how after that I didn't feel comfortable about joining Brian in doing those kinds of things anymore.

"He'd call me names, and I'd hate it because it made me feel like such a creep!"

"Oh, Tim!" Mom exclaimed.

"Brian seemed to know his way around in ways I didn't. I thought maybe kids in the East do stuff like that and it's cool. Besides, I didn't want to be tattling on him."

Mom and Dad exchanged troubled glances.

I told them the rest. About the night at the hotel in New Haven. About the gift Brian gave Mom that had no sales slip and the price still on. About the boot in our closet full of jewelry and Mom's brooch in the cup on his desk; the clippings on the robberies and the fire at the General Store; the vandalisms—including the one at school blamed on someone I was sure was innocent; the cat poisonings . . .

They interrupted with questions, and I answered, and went on telling them what Grandma told me, too.

Finally I said, "I think Brian did all of it, Mom and Dad. I think he lies and steals and sets fires and maybe even kills. I think he's dangerous and evil."

By the time I finished, Mom's eyes glistened with tears. She turned to Dad. "How could we have lived here all this time and not known what was going on? Could we have been so blind? It's true, there *was* that terrible drowning years ago, and after that your brother always gave you such vague answers about Brian. 'He's away at Chatham, or Harvard Private Academy,' or 'He's in Europe with a special study group for the summer.' We used to think Pete and Linda were too involved in their careers to give Brian time, but maybe it wasn't that at all. Maybe Brian was more than they could handle, or *anyone* could. Maybe he got thrown out of those schools!"

"Now, *wait* a *minute*!" Dad cried. "I know it doesn't look good, but you're talking like Brian's a psycho! He may have problems. But aren't you condemning him without a trial? Don't you think we should speak with *him*?"

"About what, Dad? If he did any of this? Do you think he'd admit it? He's such a good liar! You could catch him with his hand in your wallet and he'd deny it! Remember how he got around your asking about Mom's car being hot that day?"

"I'm not saying I don't believe you, Tim, but he's lived in our house two months now. He's a good student; he's neat and thoughtful. Polite. Plays with Cookie like he really loves her. Maybe he really *was* out nights playing cops and robbers. It's a foolish thing to do, to be sure, but he's a loner; it might be just the sort of thing he'd do to get attention. Barbara, have you sensed anything?"

"Not really, but now that I think about it, he's *too* accommodating, maybe a little *too* perfect. And he doesn't show any *real* emotion. Know what I mean? Even at the funeral. I thought it was shock, but he's rarely mentioned his parents since. Still, as you said, he's very good, very patient with Cookie."

"All right. He has problems. Maybe he shoplifts and maybe some other things. He's a troubled young man crying for help. I'll buy that. We'll get him help."

"It's more than that, Dad!" I interrupted, angry to hear him ignore Brian's most threatening behavior. "Brian seems to have—no *conscience*; none at all! I think he killed his own cat so no one would believe he could have poisoned all the others."

"*Now that* I don't believe. That's going too far! He was absolutely distraught when that cat lay dying!"

"I saw him when he first came into the yard, Dad! He wasn't one bit distraught. He was triumphant! It was only when he saw *you* that he put on the distraught act. Brian's weird! He's *evil*! You've got to *do* something before he hurts one of us!"

Dad shifted uncomfortably in his chair. "Let's not label him a psychopath so fast. Brian's complex, troubled, but he's your own flesh and blood, remember. We do have to do something. He's gone through a lot, and who knows what effect those deaths had on him? I'll speak to a professional. Meanwhile, let's not build this into something major. Not to say we shouldn't keep a close watch on his doings. Hopefully, we can get his problems resolved quickly." Dad cocked his head and regarded me quizzically. "Satisfied?"

"No, but do I have a choice?" Somehow, I hadn't managed to get across how really dangerous Brian was. "Just one thing," I added. "You may think Brian's wonderful with Cookie, but I don't. I wouldn't trust him alone with a goldfish. Please, Mom, whatever you do, don't leave Cookie with him for a minute. Okay?"

"If you say so." Mom stood, touched Dad's arm, then crossed the room to where I sat. She tousled my hair in a way that made me feel she hadn't taken what I said seriously enough.

I shook her off. "Mom, *promise?*"

"Yes, yes. Of course I promise. Until we're sure, I'll be watching Brian like a hawk."

"And no more secrets," Dad added. "If anything more happens that you learn about—come to me immediately!"

19

Brian glanced around the dinner table and instantly knew we'd been talking. I guess a guy like him grows special antennae to warn him of trouble. He caught Mom's forced gaiety, her avoidance of eye contact, and Dad's watchfulness. To cover for the awkwardness Brian babbled almost nonstop about his biking up the coast. Walking on the beach, picnicking in the dunes, the sunset . . . He even named the "guy" he cycled with, like an apology to me. Not Gina after all.

When Cookie went off to bed I went to my room and left the door open. Somehow, it made me feel better knowing I could hear if she needed me. Brian came up soon after, crossed the room, opened the doors to the balcony, and leaned on the railing looking out to the pool.

"You going *hunting* tonight?" I asked, referring to his nightly prowl for criminals.

He shook his head without turning.

"How come?"

"Something funny's going on around here. You guys have been talking about me behind my back. Right?" He swung around to look at me.

I felt my face get hot and bent over my book.

"Come on, cuz. Your face says it all. I can smell conspiracy a mile away. Whenever my folks were conspiring to send me away to another dumb school, I *knew*. Sixth sense. I knew tonight. You're all against me. You may as well talk because I'll find out anyway."

"All right!" I swung my chair around to face him. "I told them all about you and what Grandma said, too. What you did to the houses, the car, the cat, the robberies—everything."

You'd think he'd have been blown away, knowing he'd lost all our trust, but instead, he seemed puzzled. "You're crazy. I haven't done a thing, you know that. How can you say such awful things? I wouldn't poison my own cat!"

"You're amazing! You don't even know when you're lying!" I cried.

"I'm *not* lying!" His hands clenched into fists as he strode to the foot of my bed, sincerity written all over his face. "Why don't you like me, Tim? Is that why you're making up these stories?"

"You're *sick*, Brian, you know that? Really sick!"

Brian's eyes narrowed into dark slits. "Don't ever call me sick again, cuz. Don't ever *ever* call me that again!"

We stared at each other. Shivers ran down my spine. Then Brian smiled, changed into his dark shirt, and without another word left the room. I didn't see him for the rest of the night.

A kind of quiet fell over our house in the days after that, an uneasy quiet. When Mom had meetings, she took Cookie along, a change not lost on Brian. The talk time she and Brian used to share after school stopped, because Mom often found reasons to be away from home after school. And Brian began seeing a psychologist two afternoons a week. Dad said he had to deal with the trauma of his parents' deaths, but Brian knew the real reason.

He seemed secretly amused by it, though not in front of Dad. "I know what they're up to," he confided after one session. He tapped his head. "They want to know what goes on inside here. And that's private property."

He whistled a little tune, then stopped and added, "Bet I've been to more shrinks than I've got fingers and toes. My dad believed in those witch doctors. They think they're *so* smart. Think they're really getting into my skull." His lips curled into a lopsided grin. "They're really not very bright, you know."

When I told that to Dad he said, "Brian's wrong. They're a lot smarter than he thinks."

I hoped Dad was right.

"Dr. Moore really thinks he's making progress," I heard him tell Mom a few weeks later.

"Moore won't go into detail, but he did say that Brian seemed very bright, verbal, quite intuitive, and eager to cooperate."

Don't believe it, I thought. He's snowing the doctor, manipulating him like he did all the others.

"He does seem more relaxed, don't you think, Bill?" Mom asked. "And the crimes for the area have dropped way down in the last few weeks— not that I ever believed Brian was responsible for any of that to begin with, but . . . Do you think we misjudged him?"

"I wish I could think that, but I suspect there's something to what Tim says."

Thank you, Dad, I said, silently.

"Now be sure to be home by three," Mom said the day Grandma was due back from her trip to Japan. "Isabel should be through cleaning by two, which is when I have to leave for the airport. She's agreed to stay an extra hour to look after Cookie but not a minute longer, so be home *on time!*"

"Aren't I always? When's Brian due?" I kept my voice low because Brian hadn't come downstairs yet.

"About four. He's seeing Dr. Moore this afternoon." Mom ran a nervous hand through her hair. "Quit worrying so much. Brian's doing fine. Now, where did I put that list?" She rummaged in her purse. "Cookie? Let's go! Isabel? Be sure to put extra towels on the guest bed in Cookie's room!" She grabbed her purse and car keys and headed for the garage door just as Brian came downstairs. "See you guys later!" she called. "With Grandma!"

"Swell," Brian muttered. "I can hardly wait."

"Would you like me to come over later and *Cookie-sit* with you?" Gina asked an hour before I left school. Her lips smiled, but she looked worried. I had begun to avoid Gina when she sided too often with Brian. We saw even less of each other as I stayed around home more until I could be sure Brian wouldn't hurt my family. Gina would never go to a guy's home, so this was a huge concession, a peace offering.

"Sure," I said, feeling a surge of warmth toward her for the first time in weeks. "That would be terrific." I touched her cheek. It gave me pleasure to see the worry leave her eyes. "See you later."

Happy, I pushed through about twenty kids from the choir waiting for the elevator, when suddenly the elevator arrived and the crowd surged forward. "Hey, wait! Hey, let me by!" I cried as I was swept—no *pushed*—into the elevator while fighting to break free. "Hey, stop! Let me out!" My head felt like it would burst. I could hardly breathe. I was jammed solidly in the middle of the choir group, facing the back, as the elevator door closed. *Okay, okay, okay. It's okay* I tried to tell myself, taking deep breaths. *In a minute you'll be out of here.* Then the alarm went off, the lights went out, and the elevator jerked to a stop between floors. I stood rigid, sweating like a faucet, trying not to scream while around me kids sang, laughed, and joked. It seemed like hours before the elevator started again and the doors opened at the ground floor. Gagging, I forced my way out, rushed to the rest room, and threw up.

Had I heard Brian's voice in that mob?

It took me some time to recover, but tired and subdued, I got home a few minutes before three. "Hello! I'm home!" I called as I came in the front door. "Cookie! Isabel! I'm home!" I ran up the stairs to dump my books, then back down to the kitchen. It smelled great, full of stuff Mom had cooked for dinner tonight in Grandma's honor. I poured a glass of orange juice to clear the awful taste in my mouth and wondered where Isabel and Cookie were. Except for the washer and dryer going in the basement, the house felt empty.

I opened the door to the basement and stepped down a few stairs. "Isabel? You down there?" I listened. No answer. Shrugging, I went back to the kitchen, put the juice carton away. Mom had said Isabel couldn't stay past three. She probably took Cookie out for a walk, but they should have been back by now.

The house seemed so awfully, deadly silent.

A cold sweat gushed down my back at a sudden thought. Could I have been *pushed* into that elevator? It had delayed my getting home by a half hour. Could Brian be here? Could he have skipped his appointment? Come home before me? Told Isabel he'd take over? Sent her home?

I raced upstairs, checked Cookie's room, her closet, Mom and Dad's room and closets, the bathrooms. I ran back to my room, checked there, and threw the doors open to the balcony. Panting from a growing terror, I gripped the balcony rail and leaned over, trying to see everything in the backyard.

Where was Plato? Why didn't he bark as soon as I opened the balcony door?

Was someone sitting at the table under the umbrella? A fist clenched in my stomach. What was that shadow in the pool?

I flew down the stairs and out the back door, almost choking on the scream starting in my throat.

My eyes swept the pool. It was! It was! "Cookie!" My sister bobbed beneath the surface of the water, in the deep end. Brian sat nearby, legs crossed, calmly reading a newspaper.

"Cookie's drowning!" I cried, still not realizing. "Help me!" I dove into the pool with all my clothes on. In three hard strokes I reached Cookie, jackknifed below, and grabbed her by the shirt. Then I kicked my way to the surface, slowed by the leaden weight of my water-soaked sneakers. Gasping for breath, and clutching her with my left arm, I stroked with my right to the ladder at the deep end of the pool. I had just found my footing on the bottom rung and placed my right hand on an upper rung when through the blur of water I saw Brian's legs.

"Help!" I demanded, raising Cookie toward him. She felt so limp, so cold.

"Sure!" He reached down, grabbed a handful of my hair, lifted me a few inches, then threw me backward. I heard his laugh as I hit the water and went under, still holding my sister, gulping air and then water. When I came up again I treaded water in the middle of the pool, choking and panicked now. Brian bent toward me, hands on knees. "Need help? Come closer. Come on, wussy! Don't be afraid!"

I kicked my way around. Could I reach the other side of the pool and climb out before he could make it there? No. Could I swim down the middle and get out at the shallow end? Probably, but I'd have to fight him off before I could do anything to help Cookie. And every second counted! Plato! Where was Plato?

"Plato!" I yelled, moving slowly toward the shallow end of the pool. "Help!"

Brian watched, arms crossed, confident, amused. "Plato's gone. Free. Dogs shouldn't be locked up." He followed me down the pool, knowing what I was up to. My heart pounded against my ribs. He'd never let me leave the pool, not alive, anyway. He couldn't.

Once I reached the shallow end I slogged

toward the steps leading to the decking. Brian blocked the way. I swung about, moved a few feet away, and lay Cookie on the ground before he could reach me, then tried to hoist myself up. But Brian had darted around the pool edge, bent, and grabbed for my hair again. He pushed my head this way and that until I thought my neck would break. I snatched at his hands, trying to break free, but with no luck.

Someone was screaming. *"Brian*! What are you doing?"

It was Gina's voice. She must have come into the backyard looking for me. In that moment's distraction I flung my arms around Brian's knees. I pulled with all my might, threw him off balance, and yanked him into the pool with me.

"Gina!" I screamed. "Phone nine one one! Get help for Cookie!"

Brian rose from the pool in a rage, blowing water from his mouth and running his hands through his wet hair. "Did you see that? Did you see what he did to me?" he cried to Gina, who was running toward the house. "Tried to drown me!"

I ran to Cookie and turned her on her back. She looked so blue and still. How long had she been in the water? Was it too late to save her? I gulped back tears and went to work, calling up everything I'd learned in first aid.

Gina came back and knelt beside me. "They'll be here soon. Move over. I'll help."

"What if she doesn't make it? What if she was in the water too long?" My voice broke and I wiped away tears with the back of my arm.

"Don't even *think* that! She'll make it. Listen! The ambulance is coming! I'll go out front and show them the way."

I jammed my fist against my mouth while the paramedics took over, afraid I'd scream if I took it away. They did mouth to mouth and cardiac massage, as I'd done with Gina's help. They started an I.V. but Cookie lay there as lifeless as a doll.

"Stand back," the paramedic said. "We're going to zap her."

I buried my head in Gina's shoulder. If only I'd come home earlier—five minutes, even two minutes! If only I'd realized that Grandma's returning could set Brian off! If only . . .

"Okay, turn on the juice!" Cookie's body jumped as the sudden surge of power zapped her, but then she lay still again.

The paramedic pushed something into the I.V., waited and watched. Come on, come on! *Please* Cookie! I cried silently. I'll never be mean to you again. I'll read to you every day! I'll play with you whenever you ask. Please come back!

Still she didn't move.

"Zap her again!" the first paramedic said.

I held my breath as the shock went through Cookie's body again. At last a small, wavy line began to show on the electrocardiograph. Cookie's chest began rising and falling. Her face began turning pink.

"She's alive!" I cried. "Oh, God! She's alive!" I lifted Gina into my arms and swung her around and around. "She's alive! Oh, God, thank you! Cookie's gonna live!"

What more is there to say? During the excitement Brian had coolly gone upstairs, changed into dry clothes, and left the house. When my parents returned with Grandma, Cookie was at the hospital. She was my indisputable proof against Brian; I wished it had been otherwise.

Brian had told Cookie he'd teach her to swim so she could surprise Grandma. "But I know how," she'd told him. "Last summer I took lessons. I can swim across the pool in the shallow end!"

"But can you swim across in the deep end?" he'd asked.

"I'm afraid."

"Shame! You're a big girl now! It's easy. Besides, I'm here if you need me," he'd assured her.

Isabel hadn't wanted to leave until I got home so he hurried Cookie out to the pool as soon as she left. First, Cookie said, she'd practiced in the shallow end. Then, afraid, but wanting to please Brian, she let him lower her into the deep end and thrashed her way across the pool once. Exhausted, but joyful, she clung to the coping and asked to be taken out.

"Oh, no!" Brian had said. "Do it again!" He'd pried her fingers away and given her a push.

"Brian!" Cookie had screamed, terrified now. "But he din't listen!" Cookie explained, sobbing. "He din't!"

Brian's not living with us anymore. He's in an expensive psychiatric institution. He still swears he's innocent of everything he's been accused of. Doctors say some people are born like that—with no feeling for others, without a conscience. Some become like Brian because they weren't given love as infants.

I don't know about Brian. The psychiatrists think they may cure him eventually. I don't believe it. Brian's very smart.

Maybe smarter than they are.

ABOUT THE AUTHOR

GLORIA D. MIKLOWITZ lives in La Canada, California, and speaks frequently at schools and conferences about her work. Some of her other titles include *Standing Tall, Looking Good; Anything to Win; Goodbye Tomorrow; Close to the Edge; The War Between the Classes; The Day the Senior Class Got Married; Suddenly Super Rich;* and *Desperate Pursuit.*

SPINE-TINGLING, BONE CHILLING STORIES